PHILO:

AN EVANGELIAD.

BY THE

AUTHOR OF 'MARGARET; A TALE OF THE REAL AND IDEAL.'

BOSTON:

PHILLIPS, SAMPSON, AND COMPANY.

1850.

STEREOTYPED AT THE
BOSTON TYPE AND STEREOTYPE FOUNDRY.

PHILO:

AN EVANGELIAD.

SCENE — *A Village.*

Philo. WHERE are you going, Charles? Come, walk with me.
Charles. Of latest style of prints, my wife bade me
Get samples.
Philo. I am looking for a stranger;
A secret intimation draws me out;
It is no steamboat traveller, I ween,
But from the moon, or otherwheres. Who turned
The corner just now? Let us search the streets.

Charles. You are no dotard, Philo, yet methinks
Your words the dotard play. Why pant, as you
Were standing mast-head in a burning sun,
Watching for whales? Keep to what's palpable;
Let mysteries alone.

Philo. Therefrom may rise
Our hope.

Charles. Why this to me? I have no hope.

Philo. That you may have. The sky hath a rare glow,
And summer-showers its beauty on the world:
Might it not ray intelligence to us,
Or one of its inhabitants send forth
To visit?

Charles. Woe is me! In her de laine
To see an angel, my dear wife would swoon.
The mystery of merchants' packages
She longs to handle. You are too well bred
Philo, to disappoint a woman's wish.
Good-by; be pleasure yours, and folly too,
If such it is; and mine — to do my errand.

Philo. Beneath the trees he stands, — it must be he, —
Fast by the church. What there attracts his eye ?
No antique saints, or welkin-aping dome.
An open belfry, and four heavy walls,
Are the sum total. Let me speak to him.
Hail ! sky-descended, — such thy look imports, —
A mortal welcomes thee, as mortal may.

Gabriel. Unto a certain Philo I was sent,
Who has his lodgings hereabouts. My name
Is Gabriel.

Philo. And I am Philo called.
In vision of the night I heard of thee,
And was constrained to look for thee. The times,
Indeed, do hardly promise such a good ;
Yet this, the steadfast compass of my faith,
That Israel will be redeemed, the Fall
Reversed. In words familiar, yet
Sincerely put, I hope I see thee well.

Gabriel. The upper blue, through which I fared, was cold
And moist. Secured in our peculiar vest,

I sailed it heedless. Yonder sky appears
As years agone, when we prepared the bed
Of this great globe; not great indeed to one,
A traveller through the starry ways, and who
Has seen the central orb of all, and spent
A century exploring base of His
Appropriate seat; that dazzling, central vast,
Which mocks your science, and confounds survey;
God's own, and overviewed by God alone.
How excellent the alchemy that turns
The turbid mist and cold vacuity
To azure day, and golden purfled eve!
Such was my revery as you approached.
I came last night near the first cock-crowing;
Traversed the streets; none were abroad, no lights
From windows shone. I set me on these steps
To see the planets rise, and galaxy,
Whose creamy flood my swimmer-pinions pierced.
Philo. How gladly we had been thy host, bestowed
Our hospitality, like those of old,
With all the ardor of a modern heart!

The gospel rule will have us entertain
The stranger; we an angel too had found.
Gabriel. I have no lack. Love is my food, my bed,
And roof. Love is my wing, my impulse love,
And soul and circumstance, my joy and prayer.
In love I dwell in God, and God in me.
Not otherwise is seen the great Unseen;
And the high host of us, in love, all dwell
Together, brother, sister, cherubim.
Heaven, stars, time, place, and their inhabitants,
Subsist in love—as love itself in God—
Wherethrough these maples leaf, and those thick clouds
Their lustre draw. In love are visitors,
Attendance, ministry, and fellowship;
Sphere answering to sphere, and heart to heart,
Within the Soul of All, concentrical;
To seraph, seraph speaking, musical
And glad; inaudible to sin alone.
Truly I nothing crave, but that you love,
And mortals all; whence it shall come to pass,

That our effulgent scope shall earth comprise,
And, man into the flaming circle falling,
This human state reflect the heavenly. —
Is this a church, of which the echoing prate
Has reached our ears?

Philo. So called. Go in with me.
These are the people's seats, named pews; and there
The pulpit, our good pastor's place; above,
The choir collect: hast never heard their songs?
Our minister keeps you no distant suit;
He wells with love, and yearns for the Redemption;
His life is hid with Christ in God. His name
Hast thou not seen on the Lamb's Book? A heart
To high heroic ecstasy attuned,
He owns, great Virtue's self beholds, and turns
To the same image; 'midst tempestuous times
Our Eddystone; Christ's passion beareth he,
And scorn of hypocrites. We follow him,
Our lesser shepherd, as he Christ, the Great.
Resolved and calm, both meek and wise is he;
Of spiritual drift, and simple human ways;
In comprehension large, of liberal taste;

Loving all things, and gathering truth from all;
Sharp-set for rectitude, with frailty mild,
Stubborn to sin and hate alone. And thus
In pastures green a grateful flock is fed.
Here we commune, and sing, and pray; and here
Our fleshly tabernacle glows with light
Celestial.

Gabriel. What is that across the street?

Philo. A church.

Gabriel. Those spires below?

Philo. Are churches too.

Gabriel. Twelve candlesticks, and all in bright array?
Twelve ministers to keep the altar fires?
What quantities of love! How thronged the way
Of Life! No sin with nice precision, none
With ruffian force, shall dare attempt the place.
Thrice happy he who dwells within these walls.

Philo. Spare, Gabriel, spare; both me and all of us.
Too palpable thy veil doth make our vice;
Thy thin blade lances deeper than the quick.

In yonder gorge, that opens to the river,
I have an arbor, coolly framed of boughs
And vines ; there solitude does teach me ; there
A band of kindred spirits casual meets :
Let us go thither ; at thy ease discourse
To me of what thou wilt.

Gabriel. Of Christ 'fore all.

Philo. The preface he of all my interest.

Gabriel. When this earth's corner stone was laid, the stars
Together sang, and all we sons of God
Shouted for joy. At birth of him raised up
To be a Prince and Savior of the world,
I led the choir, the burden of whose song
Was, Peace on earth ! Good will to man ! Beguiled,
Depressed, enjeoparded by flesh and sense,
I succored him ; his bitter cup of death
With myrrh and honey dashed ; held to my heart
His throbbing temples ; wiped the laboring blood,
His pain and terror reassuring. Then,
As steel recoiling, that heroic youth,
In conscious strength arising, smiled, and turned

Himself to Calvary — new Star of hope,
Death's dread abyss illuming where it sank.
To Mary I announced the favored birth;
Chosen from the foundation of the world,
Elect and precious, with observance strict,
I marked his course. Truth, love, and holiness,
Possessed he not by measure. He waxed strong
In spirit, right and wrong discerned, and fair
And foul. God's grace investing him, he grew
In favor with the few who knew him best
A goodly countenance had he, the fruit
Of inward life; not a June morning's blush,
Or tinctured empyrean loveliness,
With his could mate, touched by immortal virtue;
Fair rose of God, in vulgar Nazareth,
Full blown. Equipped for his peculiar work,
By culture, pureness, and humility,
With fortitude, he sank beneath the world,
The world and all humanities, to raise
To heights Edenic; Messianic Atlas,
Benign subterrene fire. His mission, plan,
Idea, was Unity in Trinity;

Atonement of himself, and man, and God;
Accordance of all earthly interests;
To smooth the face of inequality;
And, by reflective, mutual furtherance,
With just restraint, the progress of the race,
And its perfection, ratify. Christ saw,
And did, what Orpheus sung, Isaiah wrote;
Carried himself with majesty proportioned,
Elaborating premises and ends, —
With sound philosophy of requisites,
And cunning choice of agents, points, and means;
The intellectual vitality
Of kindreds, continents, times, and ages,
To the roots moisture, flavor to the fruit,
To branches strength, and beauty to the whole,
He was by nature, and by force of will
He gave; the heart of total, heavenly growth,
Beating forevermore. For this same cause,
Into the world he came, that the world might
Have life, and have it more abundantly;
The massive Trunk, and corporate Head, wherein
The members grew. He was capacious, globed,

No fraction, figment, or amorphous process;
Of atmospheric freedom and embrace.
In him met Roman, Goth, and Greek, and Jew,
To whom he gave the glory God gave him,
Snatching from heaven the kindling brand for earth.
Lower he was than we, for sufferance sake,
And mortal sympathy; in that he died,
Superior: we worship him, and cast
Our crowns before, for that sublimer mood
Which plunged itself in evil, and the wave
Subdued; — what the impassive host are not
Allowed.

That fraternity he formed
Of godlike minds, and bodies luminous,
Intemerate, holy natures, called the church; —
How does it? I have travelled many a rood,
And comet stage, since the nativity.

Philo. Alas! that clew of curious search should draw
You to a field so little promising!

Gabriel. It has been whispered in our bands of Earth!

The depths ethereal resounded, Earth.
Having a scroll on which was written, Earth,
A courier, breathless, came amongst us. Down
The battlements have leaned the ransomed ones,
Toward the Earth. This speculation, What
Of Earth? doth silent work in every breast.
The seraph missionaries met to weigh
The state of things: Earth! Earth! was all their
theme.
At length, from Christ, your Savior, orders came
That I should visit Earth, to see and aid,
And smooth eventful course. I know not all
Crises are stirring, ends are not disclosed.
I must look o'er the ground, what hopes appear,
What fears dismay.
The church and state, 'tis said,
Have sold themselves to sin. — No more of this
At present. Entertain me as you will
To-day.

Philo. On yonder hill, the children keep
A rural festival. Wilt thou go there?

Gabriel. Nought pleasing more. He, whom
all homage fits,

To youthful souls did homage ; loved the dew
Of childhood ; fairest imagery of his
Own innocence, ere dried by worldliness,
Or shaken by a rude utility.
Philo. The purest coin is dulled, and sadly frayed,
In various transit through the hands of men.
But let us on ; we strike across these fields.
Here enter we the woods He loved to walk.
That is a thorn, whereof they knit his crown, —
Disgrace evolved in more than poet's bays.
Behold! the twin-flower, in treasury
Of spiritual life, casts its two ruby mites!
Did not it win his blessing ? Birds you hear ;
The thrush's tender pipe, the pewit's moan
Of penitence. From harrying ways of men,
Did dulcet wood-notes ne'er beguile his steps
Where all is calm, and tonical, he came,
And oft in forests dim, and mountains lone,
He sought amends for life's incessant waste.
Gabriel. I hear the children.
Philo. In that tuft of trees,

Beyond the brook, they sit embowered. And there,
Beneath an oak, is their collation spread,
A picnic gathering of fruits, cakes, flowers.
Gabriel. They sing.
Philo. A song their pastor teaches them.

HYMN TO JESUS.

O Son of God! thy children we;
Train us in holiness:
As thou the Father's image bore,
Thine own on us impress.

O Bread of God! our natures crave
The lost beatitude:
The Father gave thee meat unknown;
Give us thy flesh and blood.

O Vine of God! of thee bereft,
Our virtues wilt and die:
Thou wert the Father's tender care;
Shield us, when danger 's nigh.

O Word of God! thy voice we hear,
  And hail the truth divine;
To thy commandments, broad and pure,
  Our hearts and ways incline.

O Love of God! we seek to dwell
  In love, and God, and thee;
The end of woes, the end of sins,
  Shall love's perfection be.

Light of the World! our path illume;
  The shadowy fear disperse;
Shine on these realms of woe and sin;
  Undo the heavy curse.

Water of Life! our life's sweet spring,
  In us thy stream renew;
On lowly grace thy grace distil,
  Kindly as Hermon's dew.

O Shepherd! guard thy little flock;
  Keep us from strife and guile;

Serene our life ; be our life's close
  Calm as a summer isle.

O Crucified ! we share thy cross ;
  Thy passion too sustain ;
We die thy death, tc live thy life,
  And rise with thee again.

O Glorified ! thy glory breaks ;
  Our new-born spirits sing ;
Salvation cometh with the morn ;
  Hope spreads an heavenward wing.

Gabriel. 'Twould gladden you to hear the lyric choired
At the Nativity, composed by Raphael ;
The spheres our orchestra. Th' angelic tongue
Is hard to turn in English ; the refrain
Alone was caught, by one rapt seer abroad
That night, his spirit haunted with a love
For man that made him watch the times. The sound

Doth echo through the earth, but void, I fear,
And dim; — a feather drifting from our wing,
That vain and gairish faith pricks in its cap.

Philo. Our minister is a new hand at rhymes;
He rolls them off as teamsters bales of cotton;
Waits Art's more perfect day for the fine tissue.
The children quit their arbor, rife with glee;
Exchanging song for play, solemnities
With pastime alternating. Goodly sight!
The girls, in vesture white and garlands green,
Chasing the flowers through inwooded glens;
And boys, by pastoral instruction led,
Reading a bird's nest, down among the flags,
For lessons high of God's paternal care.

Gabriel. I would speak with them. — Who are you?

First Girl. Christ's child.

Gabriel. And who are you?

Second Girl. Christ's child. We all are sisters.

Gabriel. Above their age, and yet but equal to't,
Since wisdom's height is childhood's lowliness.

Philo. Prolong the catechism.

Gabriel. Why do you live?

The Girls. For perfectness and purity.

Gabriel. How live?

The Girls. Christ is our life.

Gabriel. Whither tend you?

The Girls. To God and heaven.

Gabriel. A wicked world constraining, what mean you?

The Girls. To shine as lights. The trailing arbute scents
The frosty sedge, and blooms in wastes of snow.

Gabriel. Your parents, brothers, and the foreigner,
The beggar boy, the slave, the ignorant,
The prisoner, your country's enemy, —

The Girls. We love them all. On the Caribbean coast,
The cow-tree grows 'mongst arid rocks; as rocks
'Tis dead and dry; but pricked, it yields you juice
As sweet and rich as milk. On yonder stump,
Decayed and black, these pretty bellworts grew.

We dance round and round;
  We live in harmony;
So the stars sound,
  Such God's eternity.

On Ætna sprouts the rose;
  Of none do we beware;
Children men enclose,
  A sister dwelleth every where.

Gabriel. Heaven bless you; angels keep in wardenship,
Lest on a stone you dash your feet. Again
We meet among the higher seats, where sin
And hate no more annoy, Ætnean heats
No more assail the tender buds of virtue.
Philo, I never was a child, nor felt,
Like him, the pangs of weak humanity.
Our joys are absolute, not eked from contrasts;
Within ourselves a sun. Sometimes the lot
Orbitual I affect, and would endure
The shadowy spasm, for exultation's sake,

To wheel abreast the morn. But ne'er the air
Do fishes seek; one state for them and us.
Philo. Within the forest, granite-laden teams
To a ledge wore a path, now velveted
With age and grass; let us walk there. The sun
Has dropped below the trees, and left the sky,
So cool and blue, through quivering interstice
Of overarching spray, to light the place.
In brush-wood crypts, the children's clamor dies
Eddying away. Tell me of Angelage.
Gabriel. O'er will of mortals we do not preside;
That is prerogative of God alone;
Nor sermons preach, nor life lay down, like Christ.
An influence we, like memory of youth,
That combs in sea-like, on the reef of feeling,
Charming the soul with an immortal hope.
Anon, as midnight music, we arrest
The ear of sin, and make the wanton pause;
We writhle from the skies, in maple keys;
The conscience hears our voice, in sister tones,

And hatred melts into pure human love.
We brood o'er steps of helpless orphanage,
As sunbeams flicker on that slighted moss.
All souls have guardians, that follow them,
As hopes of fathers hover round their sons.
Of nature's laws, by man so named, the gift
Is not with us to bind or loose. But this,
To-day, I have, in specialty from Christ,
To be invisible or visible,
And make you so, and traverse space and time.

Philo. The Fortunatus' cap I thank you for,—
Unless I lose my breath.

Gabriel. Lose heart, perchance.

Philo. That is fast bolted to the Rock of Ages.

Gabriel. You may see sights you do not wish to see,
And hear infernal sounds.

Philo. *Nil admirari!*
I am forearmed in virtue and reflection,
And fear not devils even.

Gabriel. I would first
Hold conference with your several clergymen.
How shall they meet?

Philo. They do not oft convene,
Except at fires, or in the shambles, or
To do the state some service ; in the name
Of Christ, their mutual Lord, they never join.
Gabriel. He, whom God vested with omnipotence,
Before whose face all wickedness should flee,
May yet unite them ; that is not my task.
Philo. There rides one in his carriage ; will you have
An introduction?
Gabriel. I will speak without;
His answer shall be free, and all unowed. —
Good sir, from Christ's behest, and in his cause,
Who sees his church embroiled, and sin prolonged,
With you, his public functioner, a word.
'Tis truth your ear would gain, important truth,
And this, without respect of persons, speaks.
Redemption eases not creation's groan;
Prophetic type no antitype discerns;
War occupies and wastes the Christian clans;
The slave's long woe no jubilee arrests;

The laborer's hire to God of Sabaoth cries;
No brotherhood of man in Christ obtains.
At least this rumor reacheth every where.
For concord, strength, and general extension,
To aid the secret life, and outward bloom,
Facilitate the coming of your Lord,—
Both you, and others of the sacred vest,
I ask to meet with me at Philo's rooms.

The Minister. Your words are weighty; and long has my heart
The burden borne. Your method 's not so clear.
Tenets of faith must lead in all reform,
Or infidelity may unawares
Possess the field, and push our end aside.

Philo. I fear for thy adventure; God help us!
Another comes; apply thyself to him.

Gabriel. Could I depend on your accord, and due
Support, in pertinence of Christ's blest cause?

Second Minister. That cause keeps Holy Mother Church in charge;
Has she commissioned you to act for her?

Good is your purpose, where the sacred seal?
Our rubrics point the way; or, otherwise,
All viperous heresy our bosom warms.
In God's own time, millennial glories rise;
Our duty is to wait on him. And yet,
In private feeling, could I help in aught
Your aims, it should be done. — I am perplexed;
Forgive my awkwardness. We meet again.

Gabriel. There is a burning sense of need; all hearts
Are throbbing as before some secret vision.
Philo, put on your cap; we will away.
What see you?

Philo. Trees, like men from battle fleeing;
Rivers cross rivers, poleward scuds the sun.

Gabriel. What now?

Philo. Luxuriant fields and sunny streams;
The forest whitens to a bed of lilies;
Unwonted birds unwonted music make;
The air is charged with rare perfumery:
Are we in heaven?

Gabriel. What sets your eye?

Philo. A man,
Beside that river's brink, a naked man;
And if my sight be not at fault, his back
Is waled and bloody. Let's observe him nearer.

The Man. Into the ocean's boundless arms, this stream
Rolls on; bear me to that great liberty.
Better devoured, on billowy freedom tossed,
Than rot, in furrows, 'neath the hands of men.
O Carolina, am I not thy son?
Run not these veins with thy most princely blood?
Why written slave? why doomed to that dread fate?
Have I not feelings, will, intelligence,
And sense of manhood, yearnings for the highest?
I cannot live; with death I sooner join
Issue than life. — Who's near?

Philo. Haste we; save him.
Hold here, my fellow; we are friends. Tell us,
What is your grief.

The Man. My master had a daughter,
Whose books I bore; and while she slept, I stole

The alphabet, and gained the printed secret.
Some years before, when she was yet a child,
These arms across a swamp did carry her,
And helped her gather jasmines. She bade me,
Whene'er I lacked, to sue to her, and she
Would humor me. Once, leaning on her book,
I saw her sigh, and in her eyes stood tears.
'Why sigh you so?' I asked. 'For truth,' she said,
'And liberty of thought; to be dissolved
'From slavery to forms, and creeds, and power
'Of bigotry.' My heart within was smote,
And I did sigh. 'What ails you, Pomp?' said she.
'Tell me your want.' 'The liberty of life,'
I answered. 'Chains are on my feet and soul;
'My being, labors, aims, gains, love, time, name,
'Are all in slavery.' 'You shall go free,'
She said, and showed the way to freedom's land.
Four nights I ran, four days in forests hid;
One hour enlargement grasped, one hour indulged
My birthright's wild extravagance; the next
Reversed the whole, and sent me back a slave.
Thrice thirteen lashes welcomed me, and wounds

Untold of insult and revenge. I sought
To be a man, and this my retribution!
I cannot bide my time; I have no time, —
It is my master's; mine, eternity
Shall be. The dogs are near, — delay me not.
The fair magnolia annoys my sight;
The thrifty cane but marks my growing wrong;
The mocking bird derides my agony.
Farewell to you, my friends, and all my woes.

Philo. He goes, too nobly great for such a plunge!

Gabriel. Behold that bubble rising from the wave;
The death gasp mounts, dilating; 'tis on fire;
A flaming wheel it rolls along the air;
It glows as if a thousand ovens burned:
We'll follow it; a meteor incensed,
It shoots athwart the land; all eyes are drawn
To it. It bursts; the blazing shreds, like hail,
Are scattered. People build a wondrous pyre,
And, lo! whips, fetters, and all instruments
And signs of slavery are cast thereon.

The volleyed pæan list, and loud huzzas.
See how the riven races close as brothers;
Hear how a continental joy explodes,
And rolls a-thundering along the earth!
Philo. Into the future thou hast borne me far;
Return we to our point, in place and time,
And with these visions let my actions rhyme.

SCENE — *Air and Earth.*

Philo. Steer we not high, but rather slant-
ingly;
Let me not lose the sight of Earth. I would
Just skim along its surface, as a swallow.
I tear a sprig from this tall pine, it smells
Of Earth, will keep the recollection fresh.
I would not be immersed in blaze of orbs,
That shall eclipse the light of that I call
My own. The Earth is damned by distancing.
In hands of poets, preachers, it fares hard,
Not to enlarge on what the devil has done.
They get so far from it, their rhetoric

Is vexed with its diminutive conceit.
They cut it loose from its own proper bond,
And hurl it darkling into ditch of hell.
'Twixt thumb and finger holding it, as boys
A seedy dandelion, to the winds
Some puff it, crying, Such is Earth! Not few
Are bent on burning it to ashes, as
If Time were an old smoker, who would deem
Our shire a trifle for his evening pipe.
I fain must own, I love the Earth: is that
A vice? Yet did not He who died for it?
I cannot see it heaved like draff away,
As refuse copper sold for some new cast.
Would that my arms were large enough to fold
It round about, or strong enough to lift
It into bed, where it might rest a while,
And, after its long troubles, get some sleep.
I'd cherish it most lover-like, anoint
Its head with gospel oil, and heal its plagues.
If Earth were one small garden, not a weed
Should grow therein; if it were one glass cup,
No alcohol should e'er be drank from it.

And if it were a gem, in crown of Him,
The King of kings, it should be set. Had I
The years of Enos, with my walking stick
I'd measure it, and rummage every nook
And corner of its four great zones. — Not quite
So fast, good Gabriel, and lower still.
Each bee-wooed flower, each trout-brook, every child
That tottles its first steps, all youthful loves,
The girls that weave for widowed motherhood,
The musical sea-cliff, and the lobster-catcher,
As well as hemispheres and nations, show
To me.

Gabriel. Lo, the Magellan Clouds, and there
The Southern Cross!

Philo. The Cross, all beautiful,—
Would it might drop to Earth; its saving gleam
Beclip the universal race! — The North,
And realms of the Ice King, before us lie;
Wild geese asleep in shadow of the Pole,
Ladies of Greenland taking tea together!

Gabriel. The tropics, — Isle of Borneo behold.

Philo. I see a tawny man up to a temple

Leading his child. Before an idol casts
The child its offering of flowers, and kneels
In prayer. Render me that heathenism.

Gabriel. 'Great God, make me wise, just, and beautiful.'

Philo. Fair Italy! 'Tis said her brilliant sky
More soft and clear makes instruments of music.
O, when shall Love be the Italian sky
Of all the world! We cross the Turkish plains
Where boys and girls are picking blackberries.
Napoleon weeping o'er the couch of Lannes!
St. Patrick driving out the snakes from Ireland,
The bell that rang the ancient Truce of God,
A Colonel at the feet of Oberlin,
The brook where hostile armies met and drank,
The youthful Theseus on his way to Crete! —

Gabriel. These pictures leaving, turn to facts. There lies
All Europe; — London, Paris, and Vienna.
Which will you visit? The English chancellor
From cabinet goes to his library.
Will you pursue, and list his thoughts? or walk

An hour with yonder poet 'mong the lakes?
Or tap at gateway of the Escurial?

Philo. I am no Sphinx. That problem European
Outpuzzles me. Please harness me to Snowdon,
And bid me hale it o'er to Anglesey.
All beautiful as Lake of Uri, now;
I look again, the lake is dry. So brim
My thoughts and hopes, and Fate's dark crags around
Are glorious; anon the water sinks,
And I am left a hideous, slimy gorge.
Ah, hopeful France! Knows she her destiny,
What she could do, what God by her would do?
Spirits of Brissot, Danton, Vergniaud!
Ye do rejoice, for ye loved liberty.
'Brothers!' I hear those martyrs say, 'withhold
'Yourselves from blood; that is inviolable;
'Once spilled, unto the uttermost it will
'Avenge itself. In fires ourselves set on,
'We fell, and fell our hopes, and were consumed.'
And, brothers mine, your armies disallow,

Do good to them that hate you, if your haters
Be seven empires fenced in triple steel;
And ye shall be God's children, who will clothe
Your non-resisting front with lightning-blast,
And to your naked virtue give your foes
As driven stubble. Revolutionize
In love, build up in gentleness; so save,
And be saved in the coming turbulence.
Take me back to my mother-land, most good,
Most bad America. Atlantic coast, —
It is a noble one. What bays, and ports,
And embouchures of streams! How fine a sight,
The ships of all the globe converging here,
Departing; on the sunny waters gleam
Their sails, like doves' wings; they, as those same
doves,
Are visiting each other's nests. The forts,
Gloomy deformities, their eagle beaks
Intrude among the doves. Ah's me! Fly high,
Above them fly; not a glimpse that way.
When I recall those engineries of hate,
I wish I were well quit of earth.

Gabriel. So soon
Unnerved! You loved the earth but yesterday,
And pledged to it most knightly constancy.
Philo. I do love it; yet there are times when love
Is treated so one wishes not to love. —
Forward! albeit my love, poor blind thing,
Moving amidst this endless cairn of evil,
Gets bruised each step, and welters all the way.
The foam of Hatteras! I hear the wail,
The pensive, lone wail of the sea-green sisters,
That tend the storm-seized, close the swimmer's eye,
And rocking watch o'er rocking sepulchres.
Land of beauty and of sorrow, hail!
Palmetto land! If with a prophet's eye,
Still with a brother's heart, I thee salute.
Where is *thy* brother, that free-hearted slave?
The Florid region lifts amain; alas!
Florid with blood of men who loved their country;
Sole true and patriot Americans.
Leap we across to Santa Rosa. Sooth,
Those savage men did love a gentle name.

The Mississippi's trifold mouth, where pours
The wealth of half the continent! What odds,
Let it go here or there, so it goes free?
And back it cometh every where.

Gabriel. Philo, your flight doth stagger. Is this air,
This southern air, too warm for you? There greens
A grove of oranges; will you have one?

Philo. Farther this way I dare not trust myself.
The line is broken; on the breach, a shape
Is sitting, thrice more terrible than Death;
Hybrid of Sin and Hell it sure might be.
Is it the Devil himself? How burn those eyes
In their black sockets! Its grinning, fleshless jaws
Crackle with merriment. A ragged cloak,
On withered shoulders, jantily is tossed,
As if some rich conceits beneath were tickling.

Gabriel. 'Tis War.

Philo. It can be nothing else; and that
Is Sin and Hell. A hundred imps are near,
As ugly as their dam, all busily
Employed, the volunteers with cartridges

4

Supplying. That satanic shape doth tip
Her red cap to our generals. Must I
Go nearer?

Gabriel. Wouldst not see the whole?

Philo. My faith
Is sprained; it cannot walk. But let me know
The worst, and hang my hope, meanwhile, on horn
Of the pale moon. How can the sun shine here?

Phantasm of War. Ha! Gabriel, thou art too late. The war
Exists, — thou'lt not blame me for pushing it.
I am distressed for thee, dear Philo; why
So sad, thy look replete with rue?

Philo. Thou art
Not devil damned, but devil glorified.

War. Thou art quite complimentary. Work on,
My daughters; never mind this driveller.
He's probably a blue light, or some sour
And disappointed bachelor, that hates
The sex. Dear Lechery, and sweet Revenge,
Thou nimble Drunkenness, nice children all,

Are ye tired? We have a good deal to do.
Once in, there is no backing out, you know.
There's Fever, she is really wearing down.
Come hither, duck; there lies a tender child
Fresh from Tabasco, where a patriot winged it; —
We gave the man a medal; — It is warm
And quivering; apply it to thy chest, —
'Twill strengthen thee.

Philo. Heaven's hottest fury on
This business crash!

War. Art troubled with weak nerves?
Come hither, Patriotism, adopted one, —
I gained her to our side, though obstinate,
And now none serves me with a better will, —
Take this young man, and dingle Office in
His ears —

Philo. Off, fiends!

War. He's surly; waste no time
With him.

Philo. O, lost, lost, lost America!
O, utterly undone! damned, damned forever!
Was wealth of worlds e'er cast so vile away!

Thy government turns out a worthless sham.
Thy history is black, as black as hell,
Nor can it e'er be written clean. Thy deeds
Heroic but eternize thy disgrace.
See yonder! Christians fight, and clergymen,
On either side, baptize the massacre;
Cross batters cross on heights of Monterey;
And hate perennial, on thy margin springs,
O Rio Grande! There are Poets too
In the piratic files. 'Tis not the cost
Dismays me, Gabriel; the enmity
Engendered here I dread, — the rupturing
Of ties that should all nations interlace,
The thrusting in of ages right in front
Of Progress, long step backward of all Good.
This precedent, where shall it find a bound?
How rapidly doth Evil culminate
At such an hour! These splintered bodies rot,
And feed a growth of everlasting curses.
These shattered houses may be built again, —
How healed the bruised heart of Mexico?
With my own country I've no sympathy

Herein ; no, not a thimblefull. A war,
A freeman's war, in aid of slavery !
Had ever strife so poor a countenance ?
For Liberty, and Love, and Holiness,
My blood should go, and wealth, to the last mill,
If such the order ; here, on Palo Alto,
I leave a tear, and bitterer was dropped
Never from mortal eyes. I would away.

Gabriel. The moon has gone ; where is your hope ? Not yet
Our journey 's ended.

Philo. God remains. O Thou
Inscrutable, my blindness bows to Thee !
My troubles shore upon thy bosom, God ;
In this thy sufferance of wrong, let not
My feeble will be harassed. Thou art just ;
But spare my country ; let returning love
Forestall the course of doom, prevent the law
Of ruin. Ope the eyes of all our rulers,
Supremest councils of the nation bring
To penitence. The people's passions wild,
And cruel selfishness, consume before

The brightness of the Coming of thy Son.
Renew the hour, lift up the prostrate times.

Gabriel. You have some hope?

Philo. Not while we tarried there.

Gabriel. Your western boundary comes into view.

Philo. There we just missed a fight; to whom be thanks,
'Twere hard to say, save it be God. Why mind
What bunting floats o'er Oregon? Nay, let
A hundred flags be twist to one tall staff,
And perched on topmost peak of that new province,
The signal bright of comity and love.
Let that be freedom's land, the land we boast,
But have not; family home of all the earth,
Fireside of nations; the Odd Fellows' Lodge
Of sultans, czars, and kings, and presidents,—
Eclecticism of governments. Let it
Become a Christian realm, where all are brothers.

Gabriel. 'Twill make us late in getting round, if you
Must moralize each league.

Philo. Our northern mete
Invisible! those Christian, restive waves
Will bide no stakes, and melt the devil's attempt
At definition. I breathe freer here.
The South I love, its clime, its fruit, its birds
That on New England summers sweetly flute;
Its people too, and their humanities;
I love their interests as much as they;
There are magnific spirits there, and thoughts
Of highest augury. But ah! there is
A system there, that double-knots those states
In curses, banefully ubiquitous,
Invisibly inclenching all our hearts,
That makes me hackle when I have gone there.
The North is not pure, but its vice, each wise
And prudent hand may clip. Authority
Does not compel to dumbness, nor is sin
The underprop of our establishment.
Reform is free, each bird sings its own song;
E'en selfishness is friable; who lists
May quit the lump he does not like. But, look!
The whole doth flatter hope, shall't not fulfil?

What breadth of tillage, grazing, mineral wild,
And navigable water! What a sky
Pavilions the great realm! Doth Venus' eye,
From the gray forehead of the night, ray out
More witchingly on any other planet?
Is not our twilight gorgeously expressed
As Saturn's rings? Know'st thou of better wheat
Than Genesee? What herds of cows, and girls
To milk them! Gabriel, it is thy wand
That brings these scenes before me. Thou hast found
My hope, a little rumpled in its fall;
I am right glad to have it back again.
In long procession pass the Scholars, fired
With a Young World's enthusiasm. Count me
Those Church spires, as a forest, moving East;
The lumbermen, transplanting woods with towns;
Blacksmiths, whose smirchy thews are sweltering
With thought; a noble host of martyr men,
A goodly company of stern protesters;
Poets, with pens that flash as burning swords;
And some greatheartedness in Mammon's guise,

With tenderness in ribald Atheism,
I see; Hope's golden arch, a rainbow dim,
Bestrides the horizon, and tearful eyes
Are brightened at the sight. There files along
The League of Universal Brotherhood;
Move quick, my friends; 'twill take a month to cross
That river. Collars of the Temperate Sons
Swarm-gleam among the hills. I am revived.
Come see me at thy leisure, Gabriel;
I shall be, by and by, completely well.

SCENE — *A River Side.*

Philo and Annie.

Philo. Dearest, my heart saluteth thee.
Annie. With all
My heart, I send the salutation back;
That heart in chidings armed for your delay,
Truly subdued by your sweet duteousness;
And yet it holds you captive at its will,
As whilom Cleopatra the great Cæsar.
Philo. I am late just twelve minutes by my watch.

Annie. The hour appointed, love doth quiet wait,
As snow-drops sleep till dawn; but overstops
It has no fitness for, or power against.
They are one's most impetuous temptations.
Therefor not scripture nor philosophy
Have made provision; they outwit all reason.
Could I pluck out my watch and tale the ticks?
Twelve minutes are suspensions twelve, the cord
Of Phædra twelve corded; 'twixt one and t'other,
The worst we choose to an uncertain best.
All yesterday you were away, and now
Behindhand. I mistrust that Angel, lest
He spoil your taste, and make you dainty.

Philo. And if I were, what should approve my choice
But you?

Annie. And if you are, whom should I love
But you? Your absence fills my void, in that
'Tis full of your extreme philanthropy.

Philo. What busied you?

Annie. Shall I rehearse the day?

To tell the whole, I got up with the sun,
And went to matins with the birds ; and next
Helped on the breakfast, set the table, ground
The coffee, herrings roasted for my father ;
Then swept the parlor, dusted down the stairs ;
Weeded my garden, read the Harbinger,
Practised the music that you sent to me ;
Then dressed for company. The afternoon,
I answered calls, and took a walk with Julia.
The evening, with the twilight and the stars,
Philo, so holy in our love, was yours.
I read your note : the marvel of your flight
Surprised, and more delighted me. I thought
Of you in your new aerostation, now
On mountains spired, now dropping into jails,
And of your soul's unbounded exercise.
And then, as onward fared the hours, and Night
Her mantle drew more close upon the earth,
And there, alone, in my still chamber sitting, —
From all the words we ever spake together,
From all the hopes we ever felt together,
What times the meadow's beauty ravished us,

What times the Sabbath's stillness soothed us,
From faithful friends, and pious parentage,
From visions that we cherish, and from fears
That harrow us, — from all, as 'twere a breeze,
Was wafted to my heart a weird emotion,
A gushing ecstasy, a melody
Of tenderness, that made me weep, oppressed
By very welling of the deepest joy.
I went to bed, that undiminished brook
Of love still gliding through me; all the night
It twinked, and babbles, with a silver tongue,
Now that its morn appears, your gentle face.

Philo. It is a circular stream, enchannelling me;
Its source and end are God. My happiness
Is all in loving, being loved, my force
And influence selectest. Hail, God's love,
And Annie's! Welcome, beauty, welcome, truth!
Would Philo's love were worthier such a love!

Annie. If strength of love could make the worthless worthy,
Then mine should make yours so.

Philo. If a pure love

Could make the strongest stronger, then should
mine
Make yours so.
Annie. Love reveals us to ourselves,
Enkindles consciousness of what we are,
And makes us multiples of what we were; —
A witched vibration up and down my frame,
A wanton tingling in my fingers' ends,
A sprite æolian breathing through my heart.
A demisemiquavering trill comes on,
When Philo's step I hear, and greets him with
A song; as Adriatic boatmen's sons
Their fathers greet, returning home at eve,
Tying the sea-note with their strepent joys.
Philo. A light-foot wayfarer is Annie's voice;
It follows me, it lights upon my ear;
My work, and thought, and solitude it haunts,
And all my sojournings; like Saadi's clay,
That, touched by roses, smelt of rose so long.
Annie. This ever was a favorite stroll, and now
Twice blest by your good company. Man's works
Improve, or misimprove, the valley through;

They cannot meddle with the water, nor
Disturb the bold, green front of yonder bluff,
Whose shadow grows no less, though otherwheres
White houses break the solemn face of nature.
And now, just as in former years I've seen,
There comes that same old, grindy, mob-cap
woman,
Out of the elfin gully, with a pail,
To dip her daily tribute from the stream.
She lives among the rocks, in that brown hut,
Whose roof the sun has much ado to find.
Behold a log driver, in his red shirt!
He whistles cheerly to his cranky craft;
Right strong he pulls to shun an eddy now,
He darts along the swift and narrow strait,
Now in the broad and temperate expanse,
Folding his trouble up, he lights his pipe
The swallows try, as we girls used to do,
To touch the water, and not wet their feet.
There goes a little steamboat, loaded deep
With shingles, eggs, and sheep, and your dear men
And women, issuing, ghostlike, from the hills,

And in the hills evanishing. I hear
The click of whetstones in the mowing far.
Beyond the fence, through half-grown corn, slow fares
The ploughman, peer and peasant, both in one.
Boys chase a muskrat to the death, not one
Of whom shall dare attempt that robin's life.
'Wherefore?' you ask; and they reply, ''Twould make
'The cows give bloody milk.' Most selfish cause,
Charles would instruct you.

Philo. Nay, 'tis ignorant
Humanity's device of mercy.

Annie. Life,
Dear Philo, all is life; but whimsical
Are its conceits, unknown its varied springs.

Philo. The odd and wicked even, lie within;
We see what we are, and what is mistake,
As reeling drunkards damn their capering beds.

Annie. Beshrew us all moralities to-day,
And let us love, and, loving, every thing
Behold with colored eyes. Let us sit here.

The bank, by careful husbandry of cows,
Is smooth as any English lawn. Be we
The barons of the hour. Let us enjoy,
Not lucubrate. Reflection 's pokerish,
Like walking on those saw-mill logs ; — step quick,
And you go safe ; to dally is to sink.
The troubled world of thought we two will cleave,
Like yonder pair of goldfinches, and sing
As we fly on, or silent move in rhythm.

Philo. In such a bleak and stormy age, our nest
How shall we build ?

Annie. This civilization, sure
Will furnish rags and straw ; in factories
There's flue enough, on nature's trees we'll fasten,
Defy the cold, and tilt in hurricanes.
Frogs purge the fountains where they dwell, 'tis said ;
Can't we live in the world and bless it too ?

Philo. The capital and labor theory
Don't vex the frogs, and they've no tailor's bills
To meet. We must change poetry for fact,
These arbors leave, the pilgrim staff resume.

Annie. Philo! why twist your cane at such a rate?
What has congealed your voice? Where tend you now?
Cannot I follow wheresoe'er you go?
Your hardship, strife, and sacrifice endure?
Your philosophic grandeur counterfeit?
Cleave to your thought, as Ruth did to Naomi?
What's poetry but fact illuminated?
All natural uses spiritually applied?
Am I a woman, — thence of none account?
I am not Charles's wife; can't I be yours,
Your thought's, your hope's, your catholic self's? What shall
I do? Expound me, — what is woman's mission?

Philo. To be herself, to grow her natural size,
Nor take a thought to add a cubit more.

Annie. That's transcendentalism. Talk sensibly.

Philo. What is man's mission?

Annie. God to glorify,
And him enjoy forever, saith the Primer.

Philo. Isn't woman's like it ?

Annie. Do they differ none ?
Your doctrine pleases me, and yet —

Philo. Yet what ?
Their end and aim go on unitedly,
Like two wings of a bird, to all completion.

Annie. I'm with you now, or you fall broken winged.

Philo. Man does his mission ; woman is herself
A mission, like the landscape. Her effect
Lies not in voting, warring, clerical oil,
But germinating grace, forth-putting virtue,
The Demosthenic force of secret worth,
And Pantheism of truth and holiness.
She gives withholding, draws by her rebuffs ;
Her figure is canorous, and her will
A hammer. Need she push, when through all crowds
She melts like quicksilver ? The Amazons,
Outwent they the blue-eyed Saxonides ?
The fairest smile that woman ever smiled,
The softest word she ever gave her lover,

The dimple in the cheek, the eyes enchanting,
The goodly-favoredness of hand or neck,
The emphasis of nerves, the shuddering pulse,
The Psyche veiled beneath the skin, the might
Of gentleness, the sovereignty of good,
Are all apostles, by God's right; their office,
To guide, reprove, enlighten, and to save;
Their field, the world, now white for harvesting.
Her mission works with her development;
Her scope to beautify whate'er she touches;
Her action is not running, nor her forte
To nod like Jove, and set the earth a shaking.
Silent she speaks, and motionless she moves,
As rocks are split by wedges of frore water.
'Tis man's undoing that makes all man's doing;
And in undoing lies whate'er we do
Woman, undone, is unprobational.
Woman in pureness still 's in Paradise.
Woman is Poetry to man's dull Prose,
The hopeful Christian to his Heathenism,
And Unity to his malign Dissent.
When she the apple plucked, she kept the juice,

And is the savoriness of all life's fruit.
If men were what they should be, woman then
Would be consorted; now she reigns alone.
For Isis and Osiris' mutual sway,
And their indissoluble crowns, we wait.

Annie. Some visit prisons, some in synods talk,
And some in rhymes, while others criticize.

Philo. If woman feels the sacred fire of genius,
Give her the liberty to genius owed.
But the world's greatness is diminutive,
And what is small the true magnificence,
And a good mother greater than a queen.
Woman is the heart of the family,
If man the head. Good families would make
Good towns, a good republic. Congress, banks,
And tariffs are outpeered by one sweet home.
Let these their destiny fulfil, and spread,
As spreads the air. Then, at the Rio Grande,
On one bank Charles should dwell, across the stream
His neighbor Carlos live, and Oregon

Would share the virtues and the wealth of Maine,
Cornelia show her sons in every house.
There's work enough for any woman, great
In character and consequence as man's.
Such my discourse, long drawn on the short text,
'To be herself, and grow her natural size.'

Annie. I shall be equal then to you.

Philo. The day
Come quickly when this twain one flesh shall be!

Annie. Charles is not happy with his wife.

Philo. Too true.
'Tis his cross; may he shoulder it with grace.

Annie. I may join you in all your traversings?
If not my mind, my heart is large as yours.

Philo. Your eyes with mine, my own have double sight;
Your feet with mine, my own have double flight.

SCENE — *The World, passim.*

Gabriel. Now use your opportunity; be wise
On intimation, let this spot forescout

The region where your Hope must straightway
march.

Philo. A princely room, or hall congressional,
With windows ample, ceiling high, and long
Extent of pillared cornice; at the side
A throne, on marble lions couched, that holds
A princely shape, fair semblance of a king.
The floor with people fills, who seem to meet
As old friends meet, exchanging smiles and bows.

Charles. There's sport here, I'll engage. Let
us advance;
But keep us, guide, intactible, or we
Shall jeopardize our hats, and Annie, here,
May lose her shawl, or possibly her heart.

Gabriel. That lofty one is the great King, and
these
His subjects. He is named Expediency.
These come to court at certain periods,
To make account, and entertainment find.

Philo. A company of Bishops, lo! with beards
Cathedral, gilded mitres, broidered gloves,
And capes all arabesqued. There clatters in

A troop of Generals, with beavers plumed,
And trenchant swords, and large display of spurs;
While scarlet-robed Judges variegate
The throng.

Charles. Behold the Politicians too;
I know them through their livery. And there
Are editors, by silver collars marked,
And officers of customs, sleek reviewers,
And sober deacons. I have seen before
Those persons; some are old, familiar faces.

Philo. Take we our places near the throne, and thence
Observe all passages. This is the hour
Of settlement. The king examines them.

Charles. Hist you! A Judge approaches; hear his story.

The King. What did you with the fellow?

The Judge. Hung him, Sire.
He was a young man, all unused to crime,
A gentle, personable, courteous youth;—
Dogs take these whimseys! 'Tis time of some one
To make example, blast this callowness

Of sentiment, give pertinence to edicts,
And dignity to counsel; while, dread Sovereign!
We stretch thy empire, and confirm the state.

Gabriel. Look through
That window.

Philo. On a plain I see a gallows,
Whereon a skeleton is swinging; near,
A hundred wolfish lips are howling, Praise!
And miscreant voices Hallelujahs blurt.
Beyond the crowd a woman sits alone, bent
Into her knees, and stiff as Niobe.

Annie. My heart misgives. Would we were home again.
I know that woman, she sells strawberries;
She is the mother of the skeleton.

Charles. Let us see the finale. 'Tis a rare chance.
Now learn of what stuff your dear world is made.

Philo. A Critic makes report.

The Critic. The man had parts,
But he was free, too free; his elegance,
The oily voice of foul incendiarism;

His rhyme well-paced; his manner forcible;
His motive, youth's Utopian dream of rights.
His swollen thought disdained the wonted bed,
And sought new channels, to our instant risk.
The King. How dealt you with him?
The Critic. Cut him down, your Grace.
He flounced and wriggled like a new-caught salmon.
The King. He felt it deeply?
The Critic. Deeply, on my troth.
I took away some quick and living flesh,
To save a general gangrene. It was best.
The King. Undoubtedly.
Gabriel. Through the next window look.
Charles. A poet, in the fens of high Parnassus;
His arms akimbo, and his jaws awry,
And the Brown Muse is stuping him with camphor.
I know his history. A rural life
Led he; a garden made his occupation,
His wife, his love; in a hand-wagon drew
His little boy; hung olive-jars in trees

For martin nests. The word of God to him
Did come, as in the wilderness to John;
At least, he thought so. Human ills inflamed
His heart. His generous numbers ran in tears,
His molten soul did trickle drops of fire.
The afflatus took him, as a thistle blow,
O'er fence of forms, and the establishment.
The lost sheep he left all to fetch again,
And undertook to bring the Right from Wrong,
As old Æneas did his father out
Of Troy. They tripped him with his fatuous load.
And there he is, a monument to all,
Who think beyond their wives and martin boxes.

Philo. A Bishop answers for his stewardship.

The Bishop. Those writers, Sire, did lacker well their doctrine,
Enforcing it with much array of proof,
And faying it to ear of worldly reason.
But what do we with rationality?

The King. Nothing, just nothing.

The Bishop. So did we presume.
Unchrismed, they ventured on to Scripture ground,

With Phaëtonic, wildest hardihood;
Prated of things Divine and Absolute; —
Are they the judges of divinity?
Talked of Humanity, as if to us
Humanity was not intrust; they culled
From History, adduced their consciences, —
Frailest, most feeble lamp of fallen man, —
Affected prophecy of Progress, —

The King. Ah!

The Bishop. Must grave Antiqueness to the Present sue,
Confess its sins, seek absolution? We
Yield up our function to those *parvenus?*
It would undo society, confound
Existing state, and order. Plausible truth
Is Satan's arch-device, whereby he leads
The silly soul astray; 'tis worse than error,
It is old heresy's disguise, and rare
Finesse. To let the notion go at large
Among the flock would never do; and so
We stamped it Infidelity, as seemed
Expedient.

The King. It was expedient.

Philo. A General, flush from the war, draws near.

The General. As you directed us, we did bombard
The town, tore up the streets, the houses fired,
To twenty churches gave a stomachful
Of Paixhan shot ; the citizens, of late
So irritating in their insolence, —
Zealous to vindicate our country's honor,
We let our faithful mortars settle with,
And slaughtered them by thousands, knowing well
How richly they the whipping had deserved,
And, too, how quick their thoughts would be inclined
To peace.

The King. Why halts my gallant officer ?

The General. In a genteelly-furnished chamber, where
Her friends had borne her, a young female lay,
Struck by our shells, her bowels gushing out.

The King. That was a pity.

The General. By her face my eye

Was seized as if some imminent alarm
Had snatched me; in that face my daughter's
rose,
Rose with dishevelled ghastness from the grave,
Where but a month before, with bitter tears,
I buried her, in primeness of her youth;
As like as my two hands.
The King. Of course, such things
Occur in every war.
The General. The semblance fair
Did foully work with me, and every ounce
Of my enburnished armor rattled on
My chilliness of muscle; when I would
Have choked the trouble off, there glided in
The father of the girl, like sheeted hell,
And looked at me; and as that Nazarene
Stung with his eye the perjured friend of his,
This father's eye did set on me, and clogged
My breathpipe, like a sudden bolted cup;
And here, within the penthouse of my ribs,
Thump, thump, my angered conscience flung,
As it would break me through.

The King. Didst thou say 'Conscience'?
Methought the word escaped thee.
The General. I said it.
The King. 'Tis slang, and most offensive to good taste.
The General. Conscience it was, my life upon it, sharp —
The King. Tut, tut! you make yourself ridiculous.
The General. Conscience!
The King. I beg of thee, my liege, don't speak so loud;
You will be heard; our enemies will triumph,
And our good cause be hagged with consciences.
The General. Conscience!!
Charles. Here is a row! His Majesty is scared.
The King. Good friends, our worthy General, so much
Exposed of late, and worn by frequent marches,
Has fallen in a fit. Remove him hence,
And kindly press his lips; he'll hurt himself
By screaming; let him be confined within

His tent; his frenzy it will wound all ears
To hear.

Philo. They bear him off; they cannot still
That voice!

Charles. Here comes a culprit to the bar;
What's in the wind?

The Bailiff. 'Tis a Come-outer, good my lord,
alive
And kicking.

A Voice. Is't an animal?

Second Voice. Ha! ha!
One of Monboddo's monkeys. See his beard.

The King. What is your name?

The Culprit. What's yours?

The King. Take off your hat.

The Culprit. Take off
Your crown.

Many Voices. Blasphemer! Crucify him!

The King. Hear,
O wretched man, thy sentence, given in sorrow;
That you be scourged with nettle stalks; your
tongue

Fed out to owls; your skin be stuffed and set
In our menagerie; your heart be pricked
On sharpest steeple of our church; your bones
Shall arm each gallant Samson of our lines,
To slay your Philistine accomplices;
To burning hell your living soul must go.—

Philo. The scene goes off like puffing smoke, and we,
Dear Annie, stand by your front gate unharmed.

Charles. That sprite deals faithfully with you, and shows
The world just as it is, by my mustache.
He pulls up mankind by the roots, and says,
'See here!' Indeed, there is no truth or right,
But only flams, and priggery, and clink
Of brazen pots. 'Tis Policy that rules
The whole. A soul is but an evil spirit,
That doth the superstitious race annoy;
They tweak it by the nose, as did that Monk.
Truth's loins are not so heavy as Craft's finger.
Make Truth your candidate, and Policy
Will beat. Expediency doth helm all movements,

All councils prompt; the pious conclave sway,
And caucus; now lifts its voice in prayer,
Now capers at a dance; now crisps the hair,
Now straightens it. The pulpit is a lime-bush,
Your statesmen fob you off, the press is but
A trap for fools, and patriotism their whip.
You shake hands, not with men, but with their
feints.
You read, not men's thoughts, but their artifice.
Texas comes in, goes out, a stalking horse,
This indignation at the wrongs of men
Is thievish, justice is the greatest cheat
Extant. Now, Philo, what the chance for you,
But Abner's death and burial? Lay down
Your crosier, take a glass of gin with me.
Annie. What shall we do?
Philo. One day there came to me
A note in your fair autograph; within,
A motto that ran thus, Hope on, hope ever;
And all enclosed in 'The Bow in the Cloud.'
Another proverb often we recite,
That darkness thickens just before the light.

SCENE — *The Woods.*

Philo. Hail, sacred groves! Hail, sylvan mercy-
seat!
With cherubim of beach and oak o'erhung.
Here breathes on us the Holy Ghost, from deep
And solemn resonance of rocks and woods.
Here earnest souls find their basilica,
Adumbrant vestiture of lowliness.
From barky pillars springs aloft a roof
Of broidered azure; here is sumptuousness
Of furniture, an altar-cloth of ferns
And berried vines, a downy couch of moss;
In cloven trunks of those old chestnuts stand
The effigies of ages dead and gone.
Curtains of living foliage conceal
Our feathered choir. There falls a light, dim, soft,
Like sheen of Hesperus on banks of snow.
Labor's harsh din, the Dam's commercial roar,
Attempered by the forest, touch our hearts
In melting moods. Come, Annie, kneel with me

In prayer; the turf our hassock, and our book
Instinctive sentiment of reverence;
God's all-pervading love be our response.
In this same temple of the winds and trees,
He chiefly prayed, He who our sins did bear.

Annie. Philo, look here! Upon a bed of leaves
A woman sleeps; some gentle lady, sooth,
Such beautiful conditions; haste and see.
The virgin's face, and Rosalie's fair hand!
Who can it be? Shall we awaken her?
What mortal anguish can have sought repose
In such a spot?

Philo. Wait! Gabriel approaches,
With sign of explication.

Annie. What is this?
No girl of my acquaintance wears a robe
Like that.

Gabriel. The Spirit of Love you behold.
She's dead asleep, nor can you waken her.

Annie. Beneath this eglantine two others lie.

Gabriel. They are Love's sister spirits, Faith and Hope.
Love, queenly leader of the Sacred Three,

Vagarious through the earth, fell heart heavy;
She made no interest, and did no good,
She said, and would be put to sleep, a time,
And times, and half a time; her sisters eke
Did supplicate the same; 'twas ours to lay
That spell upon them.

Annie. Thou'st the countercharm;
I beg of thee revive them; I would hear
The voice of Love, and learn the mystery
Of Faith and Hope.

Gabriel. Spirit of Love, arise;
A mortal love is ready for thy hour.

Spirit of Love. Is't morning, Gabriel? Has
That Day come?
You wake us soon, meseems; I just began
My dream, a dream of goodness on the earth.

Gabriel. Good Love, and fairest of all spiritual
names,
I knew thou wouldst rejoice to see these two,
An thou shouldst choose to fall asleep thereafter,—
Philo and Annie, pledged for wedlock now,
Long since to every virtue spoused, arrayed
In wedding garments when the Lord shall come.

Annie. Divinest! kiss these erring lips, and like
The altar-coal, it takes my sin away.
I'd linger in thine eyes, as night in lap
Of day; pursue thee, as a cloud the sun;
And when thou sleepest, let me be thy dream,
Philo and me! Art thou blest Mary's daughter;
And sister too of Jesus, holy one,
Begotten of the same o'ershadowing?

Love. Sweet voice, and strange as sweet! Not thus to be
Addressed, my common lot. Is the new tone
Found out, that every tongue would melodize?
Thou art the very woman of my dream,
I trow, and he was also there, and more,
Both men and women.

Annie. Our good friends, belike.

Love. 'Philo!' I like that name, it is so near
To what I am. Is the war ended? What
New signs are stirring?

Gabriel. Nay, it is not ended;
And if it were, *all* is not ended, sure.

Love. Is this thy welcome ? I will dream again.
Renew the untroubled trance, O Gabriel.

Annie. O, do not disallow our springing joys.

Gabriel. Be comforted, good Love; thou'rt waxen pale,
Paler than eighteen hundred years ago,
When we had such a fête in Heaven, and thou
Didst start for Earth, all ardent as a youth,
Singing and merrymaking all the way.
Faith's cross is sadly jagged and weather-worn.
Part of Hope's anchor too I see is gone.

Spirit of Hope. We had a dreadful gale; all Christendom
Brake loose, as if the nether fires had gone
Delirious; — my anchor dragged and parted.

Faith. I held my cross in every church, and house,
And vestry room, o'er the communion table;
They trod it under foot in broils of sect,
And knocked it from my hand with iron creeds.

Hope. Love said, Return to heaven; but I had left
One fluke.

Faith. My cross could do good service yet.
Love. I was not well received on mortal ground.
Allwheres I went, in Christ's persuasive name,
Enforcing love ; the love of man to man,
Of neighborhood to neighborhood, of sect
To sect, of party too to party, of nation
To nation. Current as the air, I would
Have swathed the earth ; from every fountain sprung,
That every man from his domestic well
Might draw his bucket full. But fear congealed
All hearts, like winter. 'Twas not hate, at first,
Or any depravation of desire.
Faith. Indeed, 'twas not. Beside these fearful ones,
At their own firesides, I have sat, and they
Disowned all spitefulness ; and earnest spake
Of how they wished to love, and how they tried
To love, how they would give all they were worth
To love, but dare not. Then I visited
The other side, and found the same sad tale —
Both parties feared to love each other.

Love. Fear
Produced itself, as echoes ; fear to hate
Did lead, as flash of lightning to a wince ;
Thence came detraction, intrigue, selfishness,
So on to rivalry and violence ;
By all reciprocally felt and done.
The Catholic the Protestant did damn,
And back damnations leaped with quick rebound.
An accidental shot was fired, and soon
Rejoined a salvo of artillery.
As show-bills, on their memories, did men
Paste their dislikes ; read them at every turn.
Uranus-like, the offspring of their souls,
Their sympathies, and unities, and trust
They buried out of sight low in the earth.
The little children heard my word with joy ;
But ere half grown, they reached the atmosphere
Of strong aversions ; so I left the church,
And taught in Sunday schools ; — 'twas sore to see
The hawks of evil swoop the fledgling virtues.
I found my scholars drafted for the army !

From wars came governments, and septs, and clans,
With slaves and dukes; official patronage,
Distressful excise, seizure of the soil, —
Here poverty, there opulence. Henceforth
Rivers were closed, and harbors walled, God's
earth
Was piquetted by engineers, and states
Were quarantined. In Austria we found
A passport requisite; 'twere easier
To get night's lodgings in the stars, than Sternburg,
Hope said. The Middle Ages we survived
As best we could. We boarded with the Dryads,
Feeding on nuts and slippery elm. At length
The Reformation, bustling with high promise.
We left the woods and hung about the Church.
Alas the day! the clash, the roil, the seam,
Were bad as ever; war of Thirty Years,
And Seven; revolutions oft revolved;
Fire, fury, in an endless chain, went round
And round, through fabric of society.
We set heart on America, and helped
The Quakers, but force worsted them, anon

7*

The Indians lost their friends; and Penn's fair city
Were better rendered by some other name.
The court of the great king, Expediency,
Once in our wandering flight did we encounter;
Then Faith herself, and Hope, gave up for lost.
And when this war broke out, I own the weakness,
It seemed as if malignancy had shrunk
The heart of man, and whetted, as a sword,
His passions; coiling, like a snake, about
The soul of national advance,
Which it would crush forever; I became
Dejected, and could not repress my sorrows.

Gabriel. Our sister, Love, a poor philosopher,
Philo, thou'lt reckon; yet in Heaven are scores
As poor; Earth is a lock whereof they find
No key.

Faith. In every human breast, withal,
There's love enough to float the Pleiades;
This I believe, as strange as 'tis; enough
To fill a city, would they draw it off,
As they have treated Lake Cochituate.

We've seen a million individual souls
That had this love, but knew not how, or feared,
To loosen it; who took my cross, and carved
Its image from the substance of their hearts,
Then hiding it, for prudence, or for shame.
Love. I would unbind humanity, dispark
These secret treasuries of love, unearth
This frightened confidence, this needful trust
Bring face to face; take off the crust from deeps,
Volcanic deeps, of pure and gentle feeling,
And let the honeyed lava overspread
The people. Burke and Robespierre had hearts
Alike, and needs, and aims; and might, as brothers,
Have taken counsel of each other, worked
In one another's gardens, knelt together
At the same shrine of universal good.
Calhoun and Garrison are one in soul,
Though in each other's eyes they see a devil.
'Twixt man and man, the State inshades itself,
Or now, the Church, perhaps; however birthed,
There is a dread of seeing what one is,
Of being what one should be, and of taking

What man himself, or God, would freely give.
When one goes forth, they run as from a ghost.
Hope. We fell one winter day upon a woodman;
His axe snapped keenly through the frozen umbrage;
His grizzly beard was tricked with icicles;
His flesh was tender as a child's; he took
Us to his lodge and stirred the fire, and spread
A blouse, whereon we sat. We talked together, —
His tough soul listened as he were encharmed;
And O! to see his face perspire, and how
His spirit came and went, was beautiful.
He said our words did shake his feelings, like
An apple-tree; the ripened fruit fell off;
And he was glad that any valued what
He was, and did, and inward grew; that there
Alone, in winter, the Beatitudes
Were precious to him, as his daily bread,
And that he had four stalwart sons, just such
As he, who worked with him, and felt with him;
Then absent hauling timber to the Lake.

Faith. There are some clergymen — I know them well —
Having Christ's image and his superscription ;
Great souls, at sea, whose coming into port
The world may look for by the first fair wind.
Hope. Dost recollect that Frenchman, who received
And treated us so kindly, owned himself
A pupil in the school of love, and hoped
That we would call and see him frequently ?
Faith. We visited a college, where were minds
On tiptoe, looking for the breaking East.
Love. How certain Theologicals replied
That we were wanton Antinomians,
Had best be off, and pelted us, and made
Us run for life, I think you've not forgotten.
Faith. Nor how a sculptor sculptured us in marble,
Nor how a poet wrote us gilt-edged sonnets ;
A preacher spake of us in metaphor,
A farmer let us ride upon his cart,
A ferryman took us gratis o'er a river,

A milliner copied us in three rag dolls,
A noble lady asked us to a party,
Because we were so pretty, so she said,
And let you kiss her baby, Love, declared
Our looks betrayed some princely lineage,
And pity 'twas our fortunes had decayed.
A little boy gave us a pint of beech-nuts;
The Sheik of Tripoli on each bestowed
A cashmere shawl; the Blackfoot Indians held
A council with us, said our word was good;
An old man told us we were smart young girls.
Now, Sister Love, do not forget these things.

Love. Dear, bright-eyed Faith, I'm not insensible
To what thou speakest, less to what thou art;
A phosphorescent root that lights the dusk
And lonesome hour. When we have cuddled down
Together in the storm, thy lively mood
Has kept us warm, and sometimes made us gay.
I've sailed upon an iceberg, till it reached
The tropics, where it melted. When will melt

These frozen nations, whose collisions dire,
And booming imminence, doth fright the earth!
The Sun of Righteousness shines cold and dull
Through wintry fogs of prevalent decline.
The best of men do button up their coats,
Increase their wood piles; there's no heat abroad.
Revivalists but make a muddy March.
Poets, will they not rise, the Prodigals,
And go unto their Father? The Nine Girls,
How long shall they supplant the Son of God,
Phœbean brooks be sought, the Well of Life
Given to cant and the conventicle?
Must Shelley's great heart perish, as a waif,
With none to save, and multitudes to tear?
We found him, like a pear in middle winter,
Neglected on the tree, stiff, shrivelled, while
His fellows lay in warm affections garnered.
We would have cheered him, but we came too late
And could no more than shrive his soul for heaven
Has Woman no more excellent device
Than gossip, worsted work, and drilling ears?
Shall the essays of Art and Eloquence

Never surpass the gelid, brittle foam,
That rises through the ice-flaws in the river?
O, would the heart of human kind refund
The pearls, and gems, and golden argosies
Absorbed within its depths! The Holy Ghost,
Christ, Beauty, Prophecies, the stars, the flowers,
The dreams of youth, and genius' affluence,
Impulse of virtue, all has man received,
The largesses of God, his new year's gifts,
To be accounted for. I pardon much,
And more extenuate. There are some things,
Here and hereafter, irremissible.
I would join man and man, fold realm in realm,
Reticulate the surface of the earth
With chains of loving minds, all hand in hand;
Give slips of heavenly bloom to every child,
While Faith and Hope should teach the culturing;
Sin-buried life exhume; with silver trump
Should be announced the Resurrection Morn;
The disembodied Soul of Goodness find
Its heaven here, new heaven promised long.—
Where now? The sky is dark, and Hope, I know,

Is tired. Shall we not sleep a while, collect
Our wandering energies, or dream, forsooth,
Merganthum-like, that shuts in lowery weather?
Annie. That may not be; thou wouldst impose regrets
Perdurable on transports of the hour.
Go hence with me, and make my home thy home.
Dear Love, have I one selfish thought, or one
Untoward character, or one impure
Respect of life, or any dissonance
Of universal harmony, I bare
My soul to thee; cleanse me throughout. Faith, Hope,
A presence most desired, come dwell with us;
Sit in my chamber, read my books, and play
To me, for ye are musical; my friends,
Not great, but good, you would be pleased to know.
Love. Annie, accepting soul, do not be pained
For us; no cold, or damp, or pestilence
Can reach us, nor doth solitude affray.
Whom we obey, in whom your ransom lies,
He had not where to lay his head. Go home;

We will see you erelong, and your good friends.
Having, you take us ; cherishing, we dwell
With you. Our spirit, not our persons, you desire.
Possessed of these, we are your guests and self,
Our essence fused in all humanity,
Our voices heard on every tongue, our eyes
Beaming from every eye, and in the street
The Loving, Faithful, Hopeful, walking, then
Vanish our forms, ourselves remain.

SCENE — *Regions below.*

Philo. I wish we had a lantern ; let me cut
A stick and use the blind man's spectacles.
Were I a practised beau, I might play off
My arts among these slime-pits to advantage.
The queachy bog is troublesome of step
As if our way were paved with sacred eggs.
The darkness deepens, deepens too the path ;
And while I guard my feet, my head is thumped ;
With juts above, and ruts below, I tire ;

The bank is full of newts, I'll not sit there. —
Ho! Gabriel, I'm fairly cast.

Gabriel. Not hurt?

Philo. This frog is hurt, or there's no obvious dint
In sevenscore pounds of doubts and fears, the which
I am. I pray thee, ease me. What place this?

Gabriel. Forward, Philo, forward.

Philo. Dost revive
In me that Florentine? A spider's nest
My face has stumbled on, or gummy gowl
That sentinels these shadows strikes athwart
My progress; — which is it? What subtile stings
Are ambushed here, that sly into my pores,
And peristaltic prickle in my skin;
Mosquito bites, or poisonful mercury? —
Dost thou take me to Hell! Ensconced in flames,
Below, see there, a dozen spectres glide!
What meanest? — I smell sulphur! — O my God!
Have we not Hell enough above! I sink,
Hold me, the ooze is hot as fire.

Gabriel. On, on.

Philo. Thou art not kind; dost not know me.
Canst think
I have a wish to see that place, converse
With Him, arch enemy of man? Must I
Behold the blistering of souls, and hear
The shrieks of exiles on the burning shores,
Eternal torments reconnoitre? Nay,
If such things be, I would not look on them.
I hoped to get to Heaven, and all my bent,
To aid some others in like hope, my eye
Veiling to sin's nefandous end. I had
As lief be damned as see another damned.

Gabriel. Be not alarmed. I'll guarantee thee
safe.
Thou saidst thou wouldst see all that should be seen.

Philo. And that I will; we seem to grope along
Through cellar of a cloud, it is so dark,
And there is little to be seen. The smell!
All horrors swarm to that one sense.

Gabriel. A door;
Pass through.

Philo. The Porter's lodge of my great dread!

I see a Form; the darkness hides its features; —
Or it's a beard? is it some strange effect
Of rancor and satanic mood of mind,
That courses down his visage as a shadow?

Gabriel. Speak to him.

Philo. Who or what art thou?

The Form. Who'm I?
I am the Devil; don't you know me, eh?
You are the first one that can say as much.

Philo. Jesu have mercy!

The Devil. I suppose I'm rough,
And quite unmannered, or I'd rise and give
You seats.

Philo. The hypocrite! Is that his way?
Hath his quick-witted hate found out new lures
And set fresh baits for man? What art thou doing?

The Devil. I'm culling hearts.

Philo. What, human hearts!

The Devil. None else.

Philo. Unto their final state dost here assort?

The Devil. Always.

Philo. Fathers and sons, the beautiful,

Dost catch at all alike, with pity none,
And no regrets?
The Devil. 'Tis all as one to me.
After a man's relations, or his looks,
I never ask. The fire makes no distinction.
Philo. Father Almighty! must I then believe
That malice, unprovoked, deliberate,
Exists? Without incentive or pretext,
In stark simplicity, hath such a place
In this thy universe? — How feelest thou
About the Fall?
The Devil. It hurt me grievously.
Philo. What moves thee to thy conduct?
The Devil. Moves me, dolt?
Must I not earn my salt? Would you starve me?
I have seen you before, and know your game,
Philo; you want to spoil my business, boy.
Philo. Defend me, Gabriel; he menaces
A blow.
The Devil. Be just with me, 'tis all I ask.
You tax on me all mischief of the earth;
If preachers bastardize, the Devil did it;

If converts fall from grace, the Devil did it;
If men make rum, besure, the Devil does it;
I'm somewhat dirty, that I own, but that's
Because they throw a deal of dirt at me.
I'm getting old, and grow a little crabbed,
But I have had rough passages in life.

Philo. As well one might, who goes round seeking what
He may devour.

The Devil. That's false.

Philo. Do you not hang
Upon the Church, feed wicked thoughts to men,
Gild Lust, fair Virtue cheapen, Saints decoy,
With Sinners covenant, and those whom God
Permits to fall take up, and have your will
With them?

The Devil. I've been in kitchens, held a chat
With servant folk; — was that bad? They gave me
Anatomies of geese and mouldy cheese.

Philo. What means this most unearthly stench?

The Devil. 'Tis genuine Christian stench, each pound of it;

There's not a Turk or Hindoo in the lot.
I call it fresh; it came in yesterday
From Vera Cruz. May be, you smell the works;
I'm trying out a batch in the next room.
Just shut the door, if you dislike the steam.

Philo. You are a devil quite original!
Did you not tempt the blessed Son of God?

The Devil. God knows I didn't, and yet I dealt with him
As has gone hard with me.

Philo. What is't you say?

The Devil. One day, my boy, my epileptic boy,
He healed, and I became his ready friend.
The boy flung palm-twigs in his way when he,
The last time, came up to the Holy City.
I, too, Hosanna cried. Our leading men,
Meanwhile, did shrug at him, and clutched their beards
As he went by, threw dust upon the Temple
Because of him, and of Beelzebub
And sorcery they whispered in our ears.
Then hurrying to the synagogue, they read

The curse of those that dared consort with him,
And blew the candles out. Scared at the dark,
The people's souls fell dark and shivery;
And when they urged his death upon our fears,
I blared out, 'Crucify him, crucify!'
Among the first of those poltroons. Erelong
I heard his pale lips cry, 'Forgive them, Father!'
And fell, as one dead, and when I awoke,
I was a wanderer upon the earth.

Philo. You are the Wandering Jew!

The Devil. They call me Devil;
I know no other name. Adultery
And murder are committed near my house,
I have no hand in't; byblows at my doors
Are left, I take them to the Hospital,
And get a curse for every one. Call me
A witness in your courts, I'd tell some things
To make you stare; they dare not do't.

Philo. Weren't you
At bottom of the Salem witchcraft?

The Devil. No:
I hid a couple of old women whom

They sought to hang. War gives me work enough,
To follow battles, cut away the hearts
Of those that fall. I am a soap-monger,
And out of human hearts an article
I manufacture said to be quite nice.
When business drives, at any time, I hire
Plenty of orphans for two cents a week
To help me. Oregon, somehow, I lost;
But Mexico is rich, what one might call
A first-rate speculation.

Philo. You have seen
Some hard times?

The Devil. In Napoleon's day, the wolves
I fought to make my portion of the spoils.

Philo. I mean, the world hasn't always used you well.

The Devil. It gets as good as't gives; there's no love lost
Between us. Preachers take me off; I draw
Their pictures here in charcoal on the wall.
I sometimes lack for kindling stuff; but soon,
They say, the Church will fall; I calculate

On getting all the lawn and pulpit cushions.
These burn like pitch. I have had gutter-fights
With swine, field-fights with army followers,
In my day; conclave-fights with cardinals,
Gate-fights with beggars, grave-fights with hyenas,
All for the spoils. You never saw me, eh?

Philo. Never.

The Devil. Charles visits me, reports the news;
He's not afraid of an old-fashioned bout;
Drinks with a relish, as he loved to drink;
He's back and edge a man, a man
Besides of principle, no whitewash there;
He speaks his mind, and gives the Devil his due.

Philo. What light like an intense but veiled fire
Appeared, as we came down the gully? What
That perspicable brimstone?

The Devil. Just below,
An iron foundry stands, and hereabouts
Are sulphur springs. The foundry goes all night,
On railroad orders. Freights are lessening,

And that, in my line, is a consideration ;
Though some folks reckon the supplies will
fail ;
There'll be less fighting. As you choose, 'tis one
To me. I mean to eat an honest crust ;
I'll not strip graves, nor injure living men.
I have a human shape, no human soul ;
If I should starve, would any care ? Tell Charles
To come, I'm getting blue. —

Philo. By leaps, not steps,
Let us retrace that most unroyal road. —
Unriddle me, instructor mine, is there
No other Devil ?

Gabriel. I have gone throughout
Creation, as a draughtsman, made survey
Of boundaries of all intelligence,
And have not seen another.

Philo. What did tempt
The Son of God ?

Gabriel. As you are tempted, so
Was he, yet with no sin. Pride, Avarice,
He put behind him.

Philo. Did not Angels fall?

Gabriel. Could Faith, or Hope, or Love, abandon God?
Or Light from the bed of the sun elope?
Shall bees their nectared cups exchange for pith
Of wormwood? Can the sparrow build her nest
Beneath the gulfy dam; ice be annealed
By fire? Shall order of the universe
Prefer confusion, yell as yells a mob,
The fair-eyed orbs each other's beauty rend,
Seraph with seraph huffishly contend?

SCENE — *Philo's Garden.*

Philo and Charles.

Charles. They've chosen you a Deacon, Philo, so
The street-tale goes.

Philo. 'Tis true, I have become
A member of the sacred staff, and hold
An office that much worthier have filled.

Charles. Your hopes, belike, are finding patronage?

Philo. They have not given up the search.

Charles. The oafs,
I pity them. Why, Deacon, be a fool?
The earth has slipped from memory of God;
'Tis full of worms; the Millerites propose
To bake it over, as a florist does.
Why not join them? Or, if you choose, preach Hell,
Wood up that fire, it may attract the moths
And vermin from society, and singe
The mischief out of them. All customs, laws,
Likings, are held by wrongs, like an old spike,
Through plank and beam they've rusted in, nor can
You draw them, haply break the head, and leave
The matter worse than if you had not touched it.
The Church is only a dog in the church,
That makes one laugh. There is no proper blood
In human arteries, but like our wines,
A high-spiced drug; and what you call a soul,
Is steam and gas, that drives the faculties,
Explodes at last, and burns itself to ashes.

Philo. Charles, this is not yourself, at least not what
You used to be, nor what you thought to be,
And more, I think, than what you love to be.
It is not language of our former days,
When we were young together, you as young
As I. A patriarchal age of gloom,
Distrust, and acidness has crept on you.
My heart is hale and thrifty ; worms indeed
Have sapped the force of yours. Let me not seem
Impertinent, or meddlesome ; but yet,
For old acquaintance's sake, and for that love
Which you have always borne to me, in name
Of virtue which I know you reverence,
For your own peace' sake, that is dear to me,
Tell me, why are you thus ? If friend to friend
May ever come, or curious concern
A secret hail, that drifts distressful by,
And go on board and ask, What cheer ? allow
It now. Your sorest points can bear these gloves,
While I in all observe the rules of tried

And utmost confidence. If you have gained
A title to concealment, fairly won,
For your own use reserved, and shelfed away,
I'll not purloin it. A man's heart, and house,
His watch and castle are ; no enemy
Can enter, nor a friend, except on summons.
When, Charles, your little girl fell sick, your
house
Was muffled deep in silence and in dread,
No living person, me, nor Annie, nor
Our Pastor would you suffer near ; and yet
Our thoughts kept sentry o'er your long distress ;
And when you buried the loved one, alone,
Without a book, or bell, or prayer, we formed
The distant sad procession, saw you close
The grave, and knew each shovelful of earth
Was taken from your heart, and our hearts ached
To fill the vacuum, with kindest words
Your shattered spirits bracing. You repulsed
All overture, you were master of yourself,
Or slave of fretful bias, thrusting us
To distance of immitigable pain.

Charles. Despair doth sometimes traitor prove
to pride,
And will, and strong intrenchments of the soul,
And yields what one's own wishes fain would keep.
I know you for a noble conqueror,
Philo, one who will not misuse success.
Now of myself; — but no, I do not like
Myself enough to give it you to taste.
Suppose a case, as your dear Parson says,
And take a hypothetic man ; let him
Be young, as all men are once in their lives ;
A juicy heart, like ripe grapes in the cluster,
Give him, and spirits mantling as a cup
Of ale, much hopefulness and sunny trust,
An intellectual thirst, æsthetic moods,
An average organism, and circumstance ;
His faith not set, but no blasphemer he.
Next, let him love a woman. 'Why?' ask you?
For love's sake, as he rationally might,
For that epiphany of mellowness,
And truth, and sanctitude, and every sort
Of pleasant thing, a young man 's fain to see

In a young woman, shining his ideal,
His rougher self revealed in her soft grace,
As smelt-catchers look picturesque in mist.
In brief, he loves her for her loveliness;
She dances finely, smiles enchantingly,
Talks gushingly, rays out like an old painting;
She plays and sings, all toppingly performed;
He sees her at a ball-room first, and then
At home; perpetual beauty reigns throughout.
He marries her, and then — what then? His wife
He finds a bigot to some creed, and slave
Of policy. An unexpected crew
Of saintly gossipers beset the house,
And she's afraid of them, and her brain teems
With sullens. Unenforced and common tests
Suffice to spoil that pretty scheme of love
And life, and he concludes that in himself
Lay his ideal, not in her, — as war
Turns out to raw recruits. The mansion, rich
With furniture, and exquisite detail
Of comfort, has a kitchen, cold, and rank,
And vixenish. She was no hypocrite;

In heyday of her love and flush of youth,
She felt what she expressed; as sailors weep
In theatres, and glass doth glisten sharp
As diamonds. Who blames her for her teeth,
Or showing them? The novelty of love,
As scattering corn from bush and barn will bring
The eager chickens chirping to your hand,
What depth she had, brought to the surface, where
It chirped a while, but when the sober hours
Of life arrived, 'twas gone. In calico,
The muslin sylphid to a dowdy shrank.
Our hypothetic man has lost his heart,
He gave it all away, without reversion,
Or lien; all his wealth in one sweet moon
Is spent, and he is poor as poor can be,
And there's no bankrupt act for his relief.
What should he do, and how behave himself?

Philo. Let 'Woman in the Nineteenth Century'
Give answer if she can.

Charles. Of whom I spake,
His being wasted, as the Indians, chills
And fever supervened of deep chagrin,

And disappointment sore. And in his mind
Rose thoughts, a mongrel tribe of questionings,
All goblin doubts and fears, nor had he power
To lay them. His vocation lost its charm,
While drink, strong drink, grew wonderfully
pleasing.
He kept his feelings to himself, as doth
The sun its spots; the sickness noiseless spread,
Until it ashened him from head to foot.
Of this pair children came, and one of them
A daughter, who, as I have understood,
That father's womanly ideal budded,
Revived the image of his former thought;
In whom the hope that he had flung away
Came back again, on his redeeming bent,
Returning grace of fallen saints, and he
Did welcome it, and month by month it grew;
His health and heart grew with it; on his knee
He rocked the vision of his youth, and heard
Its voice as from some Eden he had lost,
Until, my God! it sickened, as it caught
Infection from his breath, and in his arms

It died. Back in the crib, where it was wont
To sleep, he laid it; fell his strength, he could
Not hold it. Fleetingly, a sunbeam lit
Upon the sightless orbs of that lost bliss; —
He staggered to a chair, blind, blind as night.
This father was not mad, but calm, and cold;
He felt his veins ice up in that death shade;
The freezing of his heart went on until
It burst its socket. On his bed he lay
Beside the child, abandoned to his fate.
There flocked in dress-makers and milliners,
And monkish faces; there was ghostly gibe
Of chastisement, and just desert of sin,
With interludes of band-boxes and crape.
And, so the story goes, that brutal man
Drave off attendance and condolency,
And, maugre oh's and hem's, with his own hands
Buried his dead. Across the grave he threw
One gasp, expiring sign of manly feeling, —
That gasp did Philo echo!

Philo. Your conceit
But colors what has long been palpable,

And what, to tell the truth, all busy Fame
Has bruited as she list. So plain the fact,
It seemed a beaten track unto your heart,
Excepting that you never were at home
To callers, closeted in strong reserve.
My friendliness, and Annie's wish, ere now,
Had spoken, if such wish were not dismayed
By grimness of your desperation. We
Took note of that fair child, returning gleams
Of gladness in your countenance beheld,
And talked with one another of the good,
The happy Providence. And we have made
Our visits to the grave, where Annie set
A rose, a monthly blooming rose. Our faith
In silence of the universe, has heard
Its voice, and seen the spirit of your child
Take beauty from the beautiful of God,
As a Madonna from a Raphael,
And we could weep the blindness of your faith.
But, Charles, all is not lost, albeit the heart
Is lost. There's still a remnant. Nature lives,
And all her miracles survive, and might,

Might immarcessible of one's own substance ;
And hope some silent vestiges has left
Within your soul, gigantic vestiges,
Like those great bird tracks in the rock, that look
Not backwards, as you think, but forwards,
To that Young World of which we dream. Is not
Humanity a field worth your attempt ?
Your house and home, have they received all care
And proper thought ? Lies there no hidden good,
As gold in sterile regions most abounds ?
Herein I trespass. Is there not a God ?
And is not Jesus Christ the Son of God ?
I'll not tax you with infidelity
To-day, save that I wish you were a Christian.

Charles. I wish so too ; had I your faith, I were ;
But there the matter binds beyond your power
To ease it.

Philo. I've this right ; to criticize
Your taste ; that soap-monger, and cups with him,
What mean such things ?

Charles. You've scared that secret up !
Ha ! ha ! He is a hearty, jolly imp,

A soulless piece of flesh, that lives on pride
And ignorance of men, like Kings and Popes.
They lead, he closes up the march of evil;
That's all the difference 'twixt them and the Devil.—
But much is lost if so the heart be lost,
More than you know. In me the fire has run
So deep, the roots and utmost filaments
Are turned to ashes. You cannot expect
Corn crops, or lawns. If I grow any thing,
What but wild-lettuce shall it be? Was I
So weak? Did woman failing spoil my force?
That Siebenkas went dead before his time;
One peg alone Othello had whereon
To hang a hope. I've little wish for life,
As children loathe the breast wherefrom they once
Are rudely torn.

Philo. These premises reveal
Woman's true grandeur, and her excellence,—
Man small without her, loss of her his ruin.

Charles. I own the inference; but let that pass.—
I bear the world no ill; let me be free

To make up mouths at it; the railroad train
Roars through the wood, the cricket sits and sings,
And no whit minds it. I can whistle yet,
Guide you the course of Progress where you list.
I have a horse, well-winded, fit for gig
Or saddle; take your mode, leave me to mine.

Philo. You trifle, Charles.

Charles. Upon the cataract
The spray may frisk. Those depths of which you speak,
I dare not sound. Let me sport in the sun,
Till night comes, termless, rayless, smothering night,
That gathers me unto my child forever.

Philo. And depths there are of thought, and feeling, God,
And immortality, and earthly hopes,
Wherein I wish I could transfuse a light
And charm, that should attract you into them;
Till in yourself all greatness should revive,
And you possessed an Object worth your genius.
A miracle is less than Christ, from whom

Outflowed the miracle, as smiles from joy.
Old truth, eternal, reproduced in him,
Was new, as colors in a master's hand.
All truth he drew around him as a magnet,
Beauty and virtue deliquesced in him,
As salt in air.

Charles. Your Christ has changed somewhat;
His kingdom, sooth, 'tis sizable and strong,
Isles of the sea takes in, and part of China,
Each able bodied man its partisan,
Camp meetings arms with constables; his Book
Is slavery's palladium, and war's,
The rope o'er culprits, fire o'er sinners holds.

Philo. On Christ the deeds of a deluded world,
O Charles, lay not! Tax eyes of wine-bibbers
With blearedness, and accuse their nerves of palsy!
Christ is our eye; if we see not, the fault
Is our excessive sinfulness. That eye
Clears up apace, and lights the world, your night
Of death illuming. Let us walk among
The flowers; taste my currants; have you seen
A finer lot of peas? My aunt waits tea.

Sunshine and rain the Infidel shall share,
And Nature work her endless miracle
For him; nor from my heart shall Charles estray
Till that heart's faith he takes with him away.

SCENE — *An Arbor.*

Philo, alone.

Father in Heaven, my Father, and my God! —
For ten long years bereft of helpfulness
Of earthly parentage, that led my youth
To thee, my manhood left, with tears to me,
And orphan inexperience; sole stock
Of all my father's race, but not of virtue's;
A wanderer in love and thought and hope,
Till Thou didst send me woman's fellowship,
And margined me with many kindred souls;
Others' support, myself too weak the whiles,
Thy child still, Christ's disciple evermore;
Though oft unsteadfast to my highest faith,
Recalled by thy sweet chastisements of love; —

To Thee, my God, I come ; in lowliness
And utmost self-abandonment, to Thee
I sue without presumption, or a bold
Effrontery, which I dare not employ ;
This finite to the Infinite unfolds, —
Mote climbing in the rays of the Divine,
Whence is its power to climb, and whence its
way ; —
Narrating passages to the Omniscient,
Parling desires to the Impalpable ;
An emanation turning to its source ;
A link in being's endless chain, for hooks
Whereon it hangs, inquisitive ; adrift
On destiny, and borne beyond my depth,
Relying still with halcyon repose
On the Hand that begins, continues, ends ;
A vellum hieroglyphed by Thee, the key
Beseeching ; far removed, monadic, small,
Presuming on the ministry of Cure
Of numberless immensities ; in sense
Of need of Thee, with lively consciousness
Of some similitude to Thee ; my brain

In shadows, yet uprising to Thy light,
Inspired by thy own motions in my breast; —
Father in Heaven, my Father, and my God,
Resolve me, — Why is Evil? Whence, and
 whither?
This mystery unloose, this weary sum
Explain. Or if I may not know, give me
Submission, tranquilness of mind; the child,
In cheerfulness to go about his sports,
The man his work, replying nought. I bow
To Thee, thy darkest Providence adore,
And hedged in leaden Awfulness will smile.
My soul! is that thy voice, or voice to thee,
Breathing unarticled, and resonance
From the waves of the Universal Soul?
It is God's Wisdom speaks.

Voice of the Wisdom of God. Philo, my child,
Thy prayer I hear, thy wish before me comes.
To human weakness all cannot be known;
Humility must wait, and work, and find
Its end in doing; time resolves itself.
'Fore valor Evil fleeth; turns to Good.

I give you ears, hear; feet, walk; eyes, behold.
The Future opens as you go along,
Sufficient for itself, in weal, in woe.
Beyond the mountains I am; there are inns
For travelling souls. Go quietly to bed,
And leave the morrow's sun with me, and do
Not tie it to your window. Work as works
The ant, you shall have store in harvest time.
All is not bad that seems; Necessity
Of action, indolence misnames a curse,
Stumbling at threshold of the law of life.
Contrast is not an evil, day and night,
Summer and winter; nor is death, that veil
Of heavenly inition, raised to mortals;
Nor carnal appetite of meats and drinks;
Nor stubborn energies of mind and heart;
Existence wearieth not the grateful mind;
It is its own use, reason, and reward.
He liveth for himself, who lives for me,
God's glory lying in man's excellence;
I gave man Christ, as sinews to the horse,
And showers of rain on the new grass. I gave

Freedom to err, with choice of rectitude,
Setting before him life and death ; to sores
Self-healingness, to vice self-conservation ;
Instincts prevenient of accidents ;
Inbred dislike of wrong and cruelty,
Whence rallying voices cry for righteousness;
My Spirit gave, that blows as blows the wind.
What follows is man's own, and his to answer ;
Ask him, not me. Sin punishes itself,
The wicked fall in pits themselves have digged,
Gnashing of teeth and wailing fill the earth.
Recovery comes in Gospel of my Son,
In Holiness, and Liberty, and Love ;
The Evil dies when Good revives ; it is
Probational, and ends when this begins.
Evil is the exception, not the rule ;
'Tis incidental, not habitual.
Crimes remedy themselves or overthrow,
Calamity confirms the strength of hope ;
Weakness is quality of finite things,
And marks the progress to Infinity.
And ignorance is stimulus of knowledge,

As folly wisdom's rundle; shall the lark
Bemoan its pinions, man his littleness,
Wherefrom the dot becomes a kindling orb?
On all alike, air, dew, and azure, doled,
Shall one blame me for lack of natural good?
I called them gods to whom my word went forth,
Created gods upon the earth, to found
A Heaven there, extension of the Higher.
Their treason, quarrels, destitution, woes,
Lie at the door of their own consciences.
From the beginning, Philo, until now,
The pure in heart their God have seen. He gave
Celestial fire to all accepting souls,
And laid no curse upon the distribution;
Encompassed Earth with swords of cherubim,
Nor hath an evil thing gone into it;
His blue eye watched its sleeping and its waking,
And motherly his winds have fanned its heat;
The lonely sparrow-cry of grief and woe,
In Christian or in Heathen realms, he hears;
Renews the years of earth, and every spring
Gives it away to man, as a young bride;

The Poet's walks instars with pleasant themes;
In every oyster hides a pearl for minds
In earnest; sows the mustard-seed in souls
Of infants; furnishes each homestead lot
With the strait gate of highest purity.
The Old world God did bury to spring up,
Adorn, and bless, and satisfy the New;
He let his earthquakes plough the continents,
Slides the sun up and down, both poles to quicken.
God loves the Earth and its inhabitants;
And there are eyes, bright eyes, that watch for it,
Behold it sweeping graceful through the air,
And wave their kerchiefs to it as it passes.
God feeds the Earth with his essential life;
All being, space, and time, he cherishes;
His Spirit, weaving spheres together, veils
Itself beneath its gorgeous handiwork.
The Earth but plays its part in the great whole;
Matter assists the soul till it can go
Alone. On golden loops sustained, fly off
Atoms and orbs, truth, beauty, action, rest,
In God's safe concave whirling evermore.

New worlds appear, as clouds in a clear sky ;
Unerring laws, steel-clasped, bind all in one.
Should the Earth topple on some fatal edge,
A thousand stars would rush to rescue her.
All retardations overtake themselves.
The cycles are kind Nature's gala days,
When she prepares a dance on green of God,
Presents her children with a world or two.
Man's will, the last and noblest work of God,
Endowed with all resource and perquisite,
Set up in large munificence of good,
Must keep its own accounts, and if it run
Behind, blame not the majesty of Heaven.
'Tis pride, imperial, sacerdotal pride,
And ordinance of Force, not Christian Love,
For universal law, that ruins all.
Not man, 'tis God, still waits the better day,
While Mercy's hand is full of pardonings.
The final or the primal cause of sin
'Tis not for men to know, theirs to amend.
God keeps his secrets to himself. Between
Man and his death, Grace, Nature, multiform,

Their legions interpose. Heaven 's lost and won
By the same mode ; the ladder whereadown
Thou goest, Man ! remount ; forever it
Doth stand on sunny side of the White Cliffs.
Philo, be of good cheer ; thy work pursue ;
Enhomed in God, bring home thy Brother too.

SCENE — *Philo's Rooms.*

Philo. Good morning to you, dear and reverend sir ;
Nor less revered for that you are most dear.
One needs to calk his doors this wintry weather ;
But summer comes with you, a summer breeze
Your faith and patience ; do not ring the bell
When you call, Heaven's love as well might ring.
All thanks for that Oration, thunder-stone,
That smote the princock, puling multitude ;
And for that man, a worldling, who instructs
The Church so wisely.

The Pastor. Cyrus, heathen King,

God chose to build Jerusalem again;
'Fore him the two-leaved gate of Israel's hope
Was opened.

Philo. God anoint more Cyruses,
Or our captivity will never end!
The morning papers there; have you the heart
To read them? Recent books if you prefer;
Or will you take an apple? russetings,
From my own orchard; they've no smell of blood.

The Pastor. I am an evesdropper, and sometimes peep
About the walls of this great gloom, that now
Shuts up the nation. He, who would go in,
Must mail his courage to the teeth. I called
To idle out a thoughtful hour. To do
Is laid upon the shelf, or reads perforce
A novel; some minds, down of hope deferred,
Are physicking the singular complaint,
And keep their beds. I thought to meet our friend,
The Poet, here. Our Lawyer too, to whom,
Unlike the craft of old, a blessing 's due,
Promised that he would pass this way.

Philo. They come ; —
I know the Poet by his downy step,
The Lawyer, by the racket he gets up,
Clearing his boots of snow. Come, friends, enjoy
My fire ; an open fire I mean to keep,
Whilst that I can afford it.
The Pastor. Many teams,
With many kinds of wood, and many minds
Of sellers, hailed me on the road. Which sort,
My Deacon, would you choose, for yearly store ?
Philo. Rock-maple is the best, or yellow-birch.
Rock-maple preaching, too, I recommend ;
Green-pine, the soggy, dull, is not my taste ;
And hemlock, like a blacksmith's anvil, snaps,
And scatters spiteful flakes, that scorch and blacken,
Yielding no solid heat ; what is its use ?
The fire that Christ would kindle on the earth,
Where shall we look for it ? Is't in the Clergy ?
I honor the vocation, less the men
That fill, or try to fill it, as a snail

A stromb, too lean for their ambitious copes.
Give your idea of a Minister.

The Pastor. Christ's Minister is one possessed of Christ,
Able to reproduce that Christ in others;
He's no schismatic, to no creed subscribes;
His ordination more from Heaven than man;
Allows no government 'twixt him and God;
Seeks no patristic, but the Gospel model;
Tries legislation by the Christian law;
With the word-hammer beats down public vice;
Applies the truth as aliment of man;
Applies it likewise as a sword, to cut
All wickedness in two; no claw-back he,
But stands erect with Pauline hardihood
Before the face of fashion, sneers, and shame;
Serves not the times, but strives to rectify.
'Tis his to educate the soul, as schools
The mind; the virtues grow, as farmers corn;
In Heaven himself, uplifting thither Hell;
Baptizes less with water, as did John,
Than as his Master, with the Holy Ghost

And fire ; the spirit through the letter sees,
As through all variations of the tune
Some old familiar melody appears.
In prayer he leads the congregate desire,
As choristers a company of singers ;
By function a Reformer, not by name,
In virtue of his office, pledged to Peace,
Freedom, and Temperance, and Unity.
Parochially, his duties multiply,
To cheer the sick, and through the gloomy vale
To light the dying man, inter the dead,
Console affliction's manifold event,
Impress the sacred seal on marriage vows.
For miscellany, he is made, perchance,
Bishop of the town schools, and must inspect
His diocese. The office has no end ;
The spiritual instruction of the age,
And as successively the ages rise,
Forever needed. Ministers go forth
To sow the generations, in their course,
With God's own truth, and raise the crops for glory.

Philo. Our Pastor doth define his whereabouts;
We are here cosily together; fire
Is warm, and snow is cold. Let us discuss
This fruit, and various humanities.

The Poet. That's well; expound what is a Deacon's use?

Philo. The Deacon 's handle of his Pastor's pitcher;
And soon despatched. The Poet's turn is next.

The Pastor. The clergy deal with men, the Poet more
With things. The first are practical, the last
Ideal minds. The Minister obeys
The Sabbath bell; the Poet his own moods,
And wind and weather. Ministers attend
Their special flock, an unselected lot,
Black sheep and white. The Poet picks his men,
Preaches to distant times, and scattered ears.

Philo. Describe the Poet, as he ought to be.

The Poet. 'Twere easier far to tell you what he is.
Idealist with many sensuous wants,

A mouth-piece, having more to say than eat,
Creator, failing to transform his verse
To cash; with nerves as tender as your eye,
Convenient emery bag for the reviewers
Wherewith to scour their pedant needles; hates
An air-tight stove, but cannot buy a better;
A man like other men, — just feel and see.
His inward self is like your own, and bears
Resemblance to the inward self of all,
His greatness lying in his commonness.
From all he takes what each man deems his best,
As sketchers cull the landscape, in this wise
Acquiring admiration with the mass,
Since boors delight to see their huts in pictures.
The Poet is the man himself, that goes
A poetizing as he goes a fishing.
His function highly intellectual,
His impulse that deep love which wells for all;
His love creates, his thought refines; there is
No mystery; lift up the veil, behold!
His thirst for fame is like that of his printer, —
One writes, the other prints, the best he can.

His art, like that of hatters, lumps, and heaps
Of matted nature, to bow out in soft
And downy forms, give it a flowing motion;
Cat, otter, he makes all things shine alike.

Philo. Your Poet 's rather prosy. What had he
For breakfast?

The Poet. Heavy wheat cakes.

Philo. So I thought.

The Poet. Nay, there he was poetical; he ate
To save the feelings of his housekeeper,
Who took his grace so much to heart, she cried,
And vowed it never should be so again.
Love is the Poet's way, and truth, and life;
The irrigation of his soul, the lane,
The grassy lane whereby he entereth
The forest secrets of the universe.
The Poet presses crimson autumn leaves,
A Maying goes with flocks of lovely girls,
Is fond of balls, and used to drink champagne;
I've seen him at an ice-vent sit all day,
Angling for chubs. He's constantly at church,
Reposing bird-like on the Sabbath-tree.

Where men are quarrying granite, launching sloops,
Or grading railroads, building factories,
You find him ; the bee busy in his garden.
The friend of all, all men befriend the Poet ;
Lover of all, all things assist the Poet.
Arrows he bears, as Cupid did, and shoots
At fancies on the wing, and every night
Goes home with basket full of game. All time
Bequeathes the Poet something for his song;
The riven ages plasters he with coats
Of beauty, as a mason doth his laths ;
And makes reigns, epochs, nations, systems, schools,
Dance to his lyre, as Orpheus the bears.
Living no nearer God, indeed, than doth
The Minister ; less dragged to earth by whims
Of men and individual caprice.
So near he lives, and neighbor-like to Heaven,
He knows what's going on there, and reports
Divinity in its selectest modes.
His hearers few, and nice, dispersed like kings ;
Nor in a country town can he collect
A church-full, like your Pastor. But his day

Will come; the bell is casting even now,
Some Sabbath morn, some hushed attentive dawn
In the Young World, to ring a goodly chime,
And summon All to worship with the Poet.

Philo. Has he a trade, or is he man at large?
He is not recognized in law, I think.

The Poet. He is a shoemaker, or what you
please.

Philo. Has he no hope or fear, or thorn i' the
flesh?

The Poet. A secret there. — I knew a Poet once,
As he himself; and who could know him better? —
His secret was a woman, mystery,
Like Christ, from ages hid and generations,
Man's undeveloped and unfinished self,
His better self within himself not born.
This Poet felt his secret, yes, and saw,
Or got a glimpse at it, that made him long
For it, and long to be himself, itself.
There were bright eyes that heavenized his own;
A voice that spake to him in Pythian tones;
A bosom, ebbing, flowing, as the sea,

That made his own a child in the sweet surf;
And lips, warm lips, touched his, whereto he clung
As he would grow to them, and they should be
His mouth. It was his wont to cross a brook,
And on the farther bank, his Secret tend,
As a wild flower. There fell a drenching rain,
The brook o'erflowed, and washed the flower away.—

Philo. What then? Why pause as if our North-east winds
Had taken your breath off too? The long and short
Of your account is this,—you fell in love.
Poets, 'tis rumored, sailor-like, have loves
In every port. Why not, as we tell boys,
Jump up and take another?

The Poet. *He* could love
But one.

Philo. And what befell the paragon?

The Poet. Once more her face he saw, and only once,
Nodding in plumes, and sitting a fleet horse,

Another rider near; but on and on
That face it sped; the spur and whip were fast
Behind; — on, on, the plumes dash out of sight!
Philo. What was his after life?
The Poet. A semitone,
A noon subfusc, with cups of oxymel;
Some conscious worth dropped oil on his unrest;
There was a sense of deepest truthfulness
Whereto he moored himself, and went ashore,
And paced along that solemn-sounding strand.
Sometimes adown his lone and empty soul
Tears trilled, and clicked, as water in a cave.
But still the Poet loved, as was his nature;
He kept the image of his captive love,
And wrought on it as an ideal bust,
Invoked its aid, as Papists do their Mary's.
He loved hod-carriers, and the derrick gang,
Brought ragged children to the Sunday school;
Once, when he found one that had been in love,
As he had been, he took him by the sleeve,
With lure of pity drew his story out. —
It was a hind whose sweetheart jilted him.

Those bumpkin eyes grew liquid as a girl's,
And brightened, as a moss-tagged larch on fire.
He learned, as he had never done before,
The depth and greatness of the human heart,
And prisoned, tongueless heart of every thing;
And lives to be interpreter of all.

Philo. The Minister and Poet both have shown
Their hand. Now let the Christian statesman speak.

The Lawyer. The Statesman, as his name imports, is one
Devoted to the State's high interest;
Our laws enacts and executes; on points
Of civil controversy arbitrates;
Provides for easy, profitable flux
Of men and wares throughout the continent;
The rights of property defines, and keeps:
The miller's flowage, widow's dole, the mete
And boundary of debt and credit, rule
Of limitation, privilege of easement,
What makes a nuisance, or a cord of wood,
Standard of weights, with scores of things like these,

Are his concern, and all of large desert.
The Christian Statesman leaves Vattel for Christ,
The best civilian extant; forts discards;
With Virtue's awful face defends the land;
Concedes a penny, gains a pound in honor;
Promotes the freest trade with every port;
All War's exchequer turns to arts of Peace;
Mixes the nations, as a farmer soils,
Compounds their strength, and gets a double crop;
Extends Democracy by its own worth;
Creates demand for it, as for camellias,
By an intrinsic beauty; the old World
Is tender of as his own mother; treats
Her foibles as a wise and noble son;
Some lessons learns, much filial aid imparts.
The Christian Statesman owns God's government
Supreme and absolute; subordinates
To this all laws and requisitions; knows
No treason, save in those inhuman men
Who aid and comfort sin and wrong. He builds,
Improves, embellishes the country through,

As gentlemen their private grounds. He works
With Clergymen, and buys the Poet's book.

Philo. Now the Reformer, and whatever else
Is accessorial to our fondest hope.

The Lawyer. The Christian Statesman lays no stress on jails;
To punish is not Christian, but reform.
Whate'er restraints Reformers justify,
Their ends impose, the laws must give,—no more.

The Pastor. That all should be Reformers is my thought;
The Clergy, Statesmen, Poets, every guild,
Estate, profession, calling. The Reformer
Is inorganic in society,
No wheel in the machinery of life;
But needful as Physicians are, to cure
Diseases of the time; he heals the patient,
Then lets him loose again; and farmer-like,
After a snow, turns out to clear the roads;—
Needed, I say, as were those caverned Prophets.
But he must be regenerate in love,
Or he is false as wind, Barjesus II.

Let him not melt the candle lighting it;
Cursing the sin, he still should bless the man.
Why imitate that rabid Irish Count,
Who hated England with so dear a hate,
He killed his men for tasting English bread!
Nor let him get so far before his age
He loses sight of it, as I have seen
A locomotive, breaking from the train;
Be sure he keeps the string within his hands,
As kite-fliers do, and running raise mankind;
St. Patrick copy, who expelled the snakes,
Replenishing, meanwhile, the land with churches.
Reform 's like catching logs on a swift current, —
You cannot tow them straightway to the shore,
But with them down the stream must float a while;
By yielding draw, and gentle curves bring in.

Philo. The Painter, Architect, and Music-wright, —

The Pastor. Are demiurgic aids of the Great Day.

The pallet, chisel, clefs, are various means
Of one eternal, wonder-working life.

Let all in faith, hope, love, combine together,
As many elements make perfect weather.

SCENE — *A Village Party.*

Philo. We will repay thee for thy long sojourn
In those woods, Love, and surfeit thee with joys.
Unmask, Faith; many eyes will peep thee out,
As from a stream look up what eyes look in.
All frank and candid here, and worth inspection;
The forward chaste, the silent wear no chains.
The world departs, leaves these to innocence,
And pleasure. They are Annie's friends, and mine,
Not types or hopes, but substances and facts,
Ripe fruit, that reddens, tempting, on the tree,
To be enjoyed in hodiernal prime,
Not speculated with.

Spirit of Love. You multiply
The good and true, our mission terminates,
And we with it. Shall we decease to-night?

Philo. Not quite, I fancy. Here, belike, is what

May keep thee with us for a month or so.
At least, it is a pleasant death thou diest,
And were't prolonged, who would object? There
stands
Our Frances, by the centre-table, reading,
The light flush in her face, that regal air,
Ascendency of figure, are out-born,
And nurtured of her heart; I know her well.
Mary, in the bay-window, set aloof,
Is delicately reserved as that; withdraws
Not for pursuit, but that she loves the shade.
Edward and Julia ponder on that book
Of Hindoo plates, and talk of lands unknown.
She loves the world, and studies how to travel,
Since he will soon be master of a ship,
And take her with him out to India;
From that clime, mystic, eld, and beautiful,
The Ganges and the Brahmins, they will bring
No crumb, but heart, and rational account,
Will be themselves a life-plate seen of all.

Annie. Ellen is gone; we miss her clear black
eye,

That shut, and left a spot of night in all
The places where we used to be. O Death,
To rob a pearl from this fair rosary
That ever on the neck of Beauty hangs!

Spirit of Love. Whole rosaries Death takes, on Heaven's neck
Suspending.

Annie. Henry, this is she of whom
I told you. She would like to know my friends.

Henry. I'm glad to meet thee here.

Spirit of Love. What's thy vocation?

Henry. A farmer.

Love. What dost know?

Henry. To sow and reap.

Love. Dost thou know how to love?

Henry. Ask Sarah there.

Love. Has't any faith?

Henry. Our Pastor ask. My forte
Is working. Give me handleable stuff,
Stone-walling, shearing sheep, or grain to thresh,
And I am in my element; not used
To theorizing, but to concrete action.

I cannot dance with Philo's graceful air,
Nor he mow grass so evenly as I.
A portion of her lustre Sarah'll miss, —
What lace and curls and animated dance,
And all this rosy circumstance bestow, —
When she becomes my partner on the farm,
As willows lose their suppleness by years.
My face is brown, and hard this hand, my heart
Is vital, and my spirit free as ever.
I raise the corn, she'll make the bread, and God
The Good will bless us both; and wilt not thou,
Fair Attribute of God?

Love. Indeed I will.

Henry. I am no slave, or sectarist, believe
Myself no injurer. My farm contains
A little spring, that feeds my house and barn;
Crossing the road, the traveller doth drink
Thereof; it deepens in my neighbor's meadow,
And finds at length the all-diffusive flood.
Our sphere is small, and quite material,

Filling it well, shall we not make it glow,
As Sarah glows from inward love of me?
What more can angel or archangel do?
Our Pastor preaches thus, thus I believe.
In casting iron, flaws are filled with iron,
And flawy man shall mended be by man.

Spirit of Faith. This is delightful, Love. I have not been
So entertained for years. I spoke with Lucy,
A teacher, who asks us to see her school,
Where are a dozen being born again,
New crystals forming in the Rock of Ages,
She says.

Annie. Louisa sings; list ye the strain.

Bless, holy Love! our calm retreat;
The lily 's fair, the rose is sweet;
Than rose or lily, purer bloom
The hearts thy grace and power illume.

O Hope divine, support our souls;
The shadows fall, the thunder rolls;

When terror all the land enshrouds,
With thy blue eye disperse the clouds.

The mountain hides us from the East;
In us be living Faith increased;
The mountain from its place we fling,
Or o'er its top our vision wing.

The Poet. The supper calls us; Charlotte, go with me.

Charlotte. The Poet feeds on nectar; what cares he
For sandwiches?

The Poet. *Your* Poet a high fall
Resembles, Tequendama, for example,
Whereof the water all evaporates
Before it strikes the bottom, so 'tis said.
My Poet flows afield where people dwell,
Or pours his water from a goblet, thus;—
Or will you have a glass of lemonade?

Charlotte. I do not ask for drink, but poetry.

The Poet. And what's the difference? Consider now

This room; this table, these environments,
With lights and eyes so pleasantly combined,
As hardness and transparency in opal,
As strength and gracefulness in Philo's horse.
Red apples topped with grapes on a white cloth,
Please twofold taste; what happiness in eating!

Charlotte. Is that poetic elevation, sir?

The Poet. You have seen sheep turned out to grass in spring?

Charlotte. Worse, worse.

The Poet. Reflect on unity of food
And satisfaction, this and tranquilness.
Men rhyme for bread; so corn and song are cousins.
To give the beautiful to earth, and pence
To beggars, rolls of candy to a child,
Or plums to Charlotte,—all are poetry.

Charlotte. Here, Sukey! bring a macaroni wreath;
We'll crown our Poet!

The Poet. Julia whispers me
You'll thus commend your Poet to the poor.

Charlotte. Julia! What marvel will her tongue work next?

The Poet. She's simple as a kitten in a palace.

Charlotte. Too stately to be simple, on my word.

The Poet. Simplicity consists with stateliness,
As meekness with the Son of God.

Charlotte. My eye
No singleness invests, and I am dark.

The Poet. The Beautiful and Useful, great or small,
At Church or Balls, in Heaven or Earth, awake
The pure in heart to lyric admiration.

Charlotte. I am not pure; the gross and tangible
I fain would overmount, the Poet's aid
Solicit.

The Poet. Seek you maidens formed of musk,
Like Mahomet's? I do not deal in such.

Charlotte. Within myself I go, and drop my veil.

The Poet. Quit Annie, Philo leave, and all the world?

Charlotte. Till I am better. Give me, if you can,

A strong resolve, a steadfast prosecution,
A deeper love for all humanity.
We women, minionly with golden spoon,
Would sip the sunbeams! while within our hearts
Some vulgar selfishness or envy 's munched; —
A frank confession, sir, and sad as frank.
Let all the truth be told. Betray it not,
Or use it for its cure. This room, this talk,
Escape of woman's darkest, secret thought,
This shaking of the dust from off one's heart,
Is suffocating. Go we out of doors.
Pure Annie's purer guest, angelic Love,
Is on the portico; join we her walk.
Don't noise my wickedness. I truly doubt
If Heaven heeds the story of our plagues.
If ever I get there, I should be shamed
To have it known how vile I've been. In prayer,
For virtue, not connivency, I ask. —
In this fresh air, Love, let me walk with thee,
And tread with thee the beach of blessedness,
And wash my feet in foam of that great sea
That brings thee life and beauty from afar.

My habits, as a pot of flowers, I set
In the warm rain of thy correction. Make
My spirit constellate with thine, wherefrom
All haze and wanton flecks shall disappear.

Love. Who hath receives, who wanteth still must want.
The water rises to the Moon, the Moon
Sinks to the water; currents pass from soul
To soul, and interpass, electric-like.
The road to God is thronged with chariots
Of fire, and back and forth the swift steeds fly,
And travellers exchange their joyous greetings.
Truth crowns her champion, Duty, in the great
And dusty tournament of life; star calls
To star, and from humanity's dark depths,
The host comes goldening forth. I cannot work
For you, but let my heart lie by the side
Of yours, and both are quickened, both exult.
We sow each other's spirits; God's the crop.
I sound the Church, and where it rings, I tarry;
Its dulness frightens me away. I go
Where I'm invited; so came here to-night.

To those that bear an offering to virtue,
As children baskets to a festival,
And rest upon their loads, a helping hand
I give; the pilgrim kiss as he goes by
In journey to the promised land. Arise,
Charlotte; be of good cheer; thy faith saves thee.
Charlotte. I do believe in fealty of soul
To soul. More free the free make us, and strong
The stronger. Thy kind words are life to me;
So shall the Poet's be. — Wilt thou not spend
A week with us, and let me see thee more?
Love. Some morning I may visit thee.
Charlotte. The morning!
We have no help; I do the work. — Alas!
Forgive me *that* impurity. The soul
No sweeping knows, they say.
The Poet. As Julia does,
Render the broom poetical.
Charlotte. 'Julia!'
Again. The Mordecai still at my gate! —
I am resolved; pray for me, in me pray,
O sacred Love! Help me to make my vow,

My maiden vow to be ; above all cant,
Veneer, and silly daintiness to be.
Here let me spend my tears, and my remorse ;
In this dark hour thy mantle round me fold,
And see me safe at home, the spirit's home,
And mine. Let Julia shine as Hesperus.
As that same star looks down upon the river,
I'll look on life, and beauty see where'er
I go, in all I do ; so little things,
As bees from hives, fly up with Poet wings.

SCENE — *The Street.*

Philo and Annie.

Philo. A message came that she was dying ; let
Us haste, ere bursts that struggling preciousness
Its bars.

Annie. Dying! I watch with her to-night.

Philo. She needs
No watchers more.

Annie. Mine is the need, alas!

To gather strength from weakness such as hers,
Repose from that calm, sacred languishment.

Philo. Sheeted, impassive, will she lie to-night,
Meanwhile awakening in Heaven, where
The Angels, gentle nurses of the soul,
Will tend the new-born child that Time brings forth
Unto Eternity.

Annie. O Caroline!
O deep and awful mystery of Death!
Far off, the teeming world 'twixt me and it,
With interim of eating, drinking, marriage,
Or coming only as a plaintive strain
Amid the racketing and bright excess
Of being, — Death affrights me not. But face
To face with it, bared to its cold, keen eye,
To stand in very wind of that fell besom,
To wait the landing of the All-Unknown,
Of that deep Dread and Longing, in the dark,
To feel the purring, whiskered touch, —
This disconcerts me.

Philo. Have faith, Annie, faith,

Your old and wonted intrepidity,
The strong determination of the will,
Fashioned of fortitude and love, — and let
The terror gather, shadows multiply,
You shall be calm, self-buoyed, and softly, as
A snow-flake, drop into Eternity.
Ants wear a footpath in the flinty rock;
Through all our stubborn fears and craggy doubts,
Are little paths that lead into the Future,
Well beaten by the stress of pious feet.
Let not your heart be troubled; Christ has gone
Before; whither we know, the way we know.

Annie. The faith of Caroline is not in me
The sterling, current sense and principle
That faith should be. She had no fear of death;
Once, when she went to sleep, she said I need
Not try to wake her, for she might be dead.
Her faith was sight, and sight was faith; to God
Abandoned, yet unto herself sufficing;
Submissive, never abject; rational,
Ever of trust most absolute; she lay
An infant in the lap of Destiny,

And smiled in agonies ; prepared to die,
Most apt for life ; so holy and so glad,
As she had travelled on that road before,
Or went a princess to receive her crown.
I knew too she must die, and that event
Has daily threatened ; but its coming tries
My best assurance, all my thought unsettles.
I fain would weep, an I were in my chamber.

Philo. Let not perplexity impede our step ;
We shall be tardy at the great occasion.

Annie. Ah ! Philo, how the road is filled with men
And teams, the crossings choked ! what unconcern
Of this sad hour ! And we must hurry on,
Bear death and great eternity through all
This crowd ; move cheerful too, and quietly
As flows the river 'neath the din, and dust,
And creaking of the bridge. Some barter wares,
Some sport swift horses ; yonder ale-bench shakes
With vile carousals.

Philo. Death, anon, must come
To all, and tears shall macerate

Each hardened cheek of this vain multitude.
When you are dancing, by and by, that fop,
Wilted with grief, will lean upon an urn.
All days are some one's black day ; this is ours,
To-morrow theirs. The 'Cap and Bells' will drive
The boys from window where his child is dying.
We judge too harshly of our fellow-men ;
The stonyheartedest must pliant yield,
The meretricious I have seen in weeds.
God give, that death in sin, and the last breath
Of spiritual desire, and carrion souls,
The ghastliness of fraud and violence,
Would waken sentiment, and make men weep!

Annie. I see the house ; it seems in some dream-change,
As if it had its substance in enchantment.
The light about it shimmers strangely ; and
The door, — I never went through such a door,
Where one was dying! Is it Heaven invests
The spot? or my entranced thought? or some
Repressless terror? Julia enters, soft
And bowed, as if she climbed the twilight slope,

And ventured cross the line, the mystic line,
Where meet the empires of Supernal Day,
And Night profoundest. See, those maple leaves
Before the gate, frost-touched, are falling fast;
Transparent at their close, as she we mourn.
Watch that one, bright as if the sun had wept
It on her bier; it sinks, but hesitates
To drop; whirled across the street, the weeds
Arrest its course, and in the hollows 'twill
Dissolve, and smoke-like vanish into nought.

Philo. Forbear, my love; thy mind is overcast;
Wait on the Lord, the cloud will soon be past.

SCENE — *The Chamber of the Dying.*

The Pastor and other Friends.

The Pastor. We meet in soberness, but not despair;
Above the gloomy grave our hope ascends
E'en as the Moon above the silent mountains.
These partings are re-unions in the skies;

To that great company of holy ones
She goes, and we, my friends, how soon, shall follow!
In shadowy void, betwixt two worlds we stand;
The distant All-Light opes its wicker gate,
The Future beams auroral, flesh expires,
The soul begins its perfect day. Our eyes
Could not endure the beauty of the blest;
A vision veiled, as if the promise burned
In alabaster, is the bliss of those
That die in Christ. These parents weep, and sisters,
And all of us may weep; our tears are fond
Affection's vein that bleeds in severing.
Yet murmur not, soft be your mourning woes.
The bread receive, and cup, our dying Lord's
Remembrancer, his life and death vouchsafed
For us. Erelong, anew we eat and drink
In kingdom of his glory. Let us pray. —
To thee, O Father, we the loved one yield;
Thy love receive the best that ours can give,
Thy care fulfil what our poor guidance missed;

From thee begun, to thee returns the soul ;
By Christ atoned with thee, and by his truth
Delivered from the chains and taint of sin,
This purity doth seek its own ; to thee,
O Father, cometh, thine to thee. O Life
Immortal ! now endue this mortal life.
Ye Holy Fires ! absorb the quivering flame.
Thou God all glorious, glorify thy child !

Julia, (kneeling.)

Speak to me, Caroline, by word or sign,
Or pressure of the hand, a blessing give ;
Bequeathe a solace. Ellen dear has gone ;
Our numbers thin, and worldliness augments ;
We buried her in blossom of her youth ;
Still fades the flower, while ripening buds have worms
I' the root. From thy departing life, I pluck
A bloom to shine forever on my path.
In valediction, do but syllable
Our hope ; withdrawing, leave thy o'er-sweet smile
Behind ; in last exhaustion, if thou canst,
Suggest what shall enure to us for good.

Caroline. The Cross is all my stay, — it must be borne ;
Bear it well, at the last it will bear thee.
Or if you faint, you shall be strengthened ; nail
To it your sins, unloose the worst of loads.
Christ live, and life all beautiful is yours ;
Christ plant, and everlasting flowers are ye.
Be earnest in your ways, to reason true,
Frivolity and superstition shun.
Attain the resurrection now from sin,
From grace to glory mount each passing day.
Beloved ones, let me see your faces. Mary,
Thou weepest ; God love thee for thy fond heart !
The stars I've wantoned in, and fed my thought
On balmy spring, and grace derived from moon-beams.
Bring me that morning, girls, we once enjoyed
Together ; sing to me the robin, Annie,
Your elm-tree robin ; spiritual hours,
And every gentle feeling, chant to me.
Earth's songs shall cheer my Advent into Heaven.
The All-Glory envelops you, weep not ;

The Supersolar ray constrains my breath ;
The Inapproachable approaches me.

Ministering Angel. The veil uplifts ; Infinity 's ajar ;
And Christ is by ; what fears the novice now ?
God's love is still our road ; yet higher climb. —
I long have gone upon her steps, and when
She slept, have kept the charm of her pure life,
Vibrations of the Universal Love
Directing to her ear ; I rung the bell
Of conscience to arouse her heed, and oft
Stirred soothing herbs into her cups of grief,
And when her thoughts grew dark, I set a lamp
Beside her. — Ceased the fluttering breath, her pulse
Is still, forth breaks the spirit from the flesh.
Fond flesh ! 'Tis yours, O sobbing company,
To bury, yours with rue and rosemary
To cover. Preciously emburthened, I
Depart. Forever burns the Beautiful
In your night-faring sorrows, as a star :
Burns she amidst the Beautiful afar.

SCENE — *A Steamboat.*

Philo. How seemed the Anniversaries to thee?
Or were they real so they could not seem?
Spirit of Love. An earnest song, with many
mighty throats,
But all on different pitch.
Spirit of Faith. They are the sign
Of something better.
Love. Signs are getting cheap;
One tires of indications, mouth-made hopes,
When need of action 's so importunate.
Spirit of Hope. You do not tire of me?
Love. No, dearest, no.
Heaven lodged its pink in you; the earth may fail,
There still is Heaven with you.
Faith. I never was
In such a crowd. To every church, and hall,
Philo would have me go. And once in haste
To reach a meeting, brushing through the men
And women, throng of hurried fervency,

Platoons of them, that glutted all the flag,
And as a herd of famished deer, did win
The narrow vestibule, and flighty stairs, —
I lost my cross, and it were lost for aye,
Beneath the scuffle of those zealous feet;
But one recovered it, a blond-haired girl,
Who said 'twas pity *that* should miss the Week.

Love. The bright side of this many-sided world,
Our sprightly sister hunts for till she finds.

Philo. The dissonance of which you speak is strife
For Right and Truth, the strife of minds not clear
In all they ask; Columbus-like, they sail
For some new land, not knowing where to steer.

The Pastor. The world, or church has never yet desired
The Absolute and the Divine. And now,
As That Day comes, and new ideas, like
A sun at midnight, break upon the mind,
Our eyes not yet familiar with the light,
In catching at a truth, we sometimes grasp
A brother's throat.

Philo. New thoughts, new forms, like birds,
Are the most noisy when they first appear;
And blest Reform is a cold shower-bath,
Till one gets used to it. The West goes down
Before the East has fairly risen, whence
A twilight that arouses all the frogs.

Faith. Christ's Judgment hour doth verily approach,
The Bridegroom's cry is heard in all the land;
And men are out with lamps, or else what mean
The solemn gatherings of late? To-night
This bulky Boat is crammed with restive thought,
And each man, like the shaft, doth throb and heave,
As he were some all-forceful enginery.

Love. Christ had no press, or daily mail, or clerk,
Employed no treasurer but Judas; hired
No chapels, used no arts of eloquence;
He loved, taught love, lived love, and wooed earth's harsh
And grating sounds to harmony by love.

Philo. We patient wait till Christ shall be revealed
In all heart's pulse, in every movement move.
Hope. The City's beauty ravishes my sight;
Like Heaven's distant splendor, dome, spires, roofs,
Are buried in a blaze of sunset glory;
As wings of brooding immortality,
The violet beams enfold the horizon,
A golden inundation sweeps the hills;
On either side, the shore extends its arms,
Runs after us with both hands full of trees,
And cottages, and gardens.
Philo. Yonder large
And marble edifice is for the Blind;
And that, the Monument of Bunker Hill.
Charles. A glorious battle; do not touch that subject.
Love. That war, that famed and boastful war, confirmed
The taste, and brightened the excuse, of blood,
Smothered the loving heart that else had beat

From shore to shore of the wide sea. No force
Of mind, or free-born aim did it create,
Or add a drop of water to your harbors,
Or spark of virtue to the character.
The soil was good, and iron strong, before
As since, and ink as black, and gold as golden,
And God has undergone no revolutions.

Annie. I feel the sea-swell; we have left the bay,
And plunge into the boundless, dizzy realm
Of surges, boundless as our hopes; gray night
Doth thicken on the spumy vision, fear-like.

Philo. Shall we not go below?

Faith. The stars are dawning,
The beacon lights begin to gleam.

Annie. The breeze
Is cool; the week's beteeming observation
Has spent me. Let me be refreshed a while;
The City 's out of sight, the capes grow dim.

Love. The rocking of the boat disturbs me not.

Annie. Make me a stoic too to ills marine.
How shouldst thou like to be invisible,
And haunt to-night that City?

Love. Let it sleep;
Its agitation has been like the sea's.
An isle in that rough sea was the Collation.
Like children of the sunny isle were those
Who met in that great room. On grassy banks,
In healthfulness and heartfulness, they ate
And drank, and sung and spoke; and every way
Faith turned her head to catch the silver tones.
One gentleman gave Hope a sprig of flowers.

Annie. What was thy thought?

Love. I wished, and how I wished!
That such a festival were magnified,
And to the Common every sect would bring
Its table, all luxuriate in love,
The roses, white and red of conflict long,
And vile religious enmities, be tied
In beautiful bouquets of fellowship!

Philo. As clouds, and to their windows doves,
God grant
We all may flow together, and be enlarged;
From Sheba come, and Midian, and Epha!
Annie, the last faint streak of day goes off;

But in the gathering night, our love is clear
And blithe; and as we travel darkly on,
We leave a pearly, singing wake behind.
Adieu, dear City! with thy martyr legions,
And all in thee to trust, or make afraid.
We part in peace; the ceaseless wave break soft
On thy prophetic shores, lull thy repose,
And give thee pleasant dreams to-night!
Charles. Ho! Philo,
And all of you, come to the cabin; there
Is what will suit you.
Philo. What a mess is this!
Some one harangues the multitude.
The Speaker. Give me
The handling of these subjects; I can tell
Some things to cure your sea-sickness, if so
You want to know.
Philo. I've heard that voice before.
Annie. His chin is bushy as his head, and red
His eyes as ferret's.
Philo. It's the Devil; he
Of whom I told you.

Annie. What, the Wandering Jew?
How earnest! Can it be that greedy wretch?
Charles. I brought him to the meetings to convert
Him; he has gone to all, and now comes out
A crack Reformer; hear him, and confess,
Philo, you owe me one.
The Devil. My good friends all!
I call ye friends, because ye do not mind
My coarse, rough speech; I am not used to talk
To ladies; hope they will not be offended;
Ye do not understand this matter; I
Have some advantage in respect of facts.
Ye only prick a pin in public sores;
More years than you can seconds count, I've lived
In very eye and kernel of them, and
Could tell your pretty orators some things
Would shake their fingers till those rings fell off,
And make the city coxcombs roar, Reform!
Of dungeons, galleys, stakes, and battle fields,
And aches, and wrongs, and groans, of empires grand,
With all their people, like an omnibus,

Into the gutter overturned. I saw
Old Rome ; and Athens, as but yesterday,
I call to mind, and how the citizens
With flags and shouts to the Acropolis
Did crowd, when Pericles from Samos came.
I've heard shrieks ages long, and one might think
The blubbering sea a sewer of human brine,
If he had seen as many cry as I have.
To tell the truth, I traded once in tears,
Employed a hundred men in gathering them,
And sold them to the Great Ones for cosmetics.
I've looked on frozen carcasses of babies
Piled up, like venison on a hunter's pung :
'Twas in the Northern wars. There never rose
The day when to the hilt I could not thrust
My cane in human agonies. These hands
Have held hearts, dead men's hearts, all in a twist
With torture ; some on which distress had grown
In bunches like a carbuncle. I could
Take scoundrels up, as by the tail a snake,
And show them you, if you desire to see.
'*I am not nice!*'—not like your plumed ones, no,
Who bang dove-bosomed girls, as egg-shells smashed,

And cackle of the deed, disnatured pullets!
For months; — I've seen it done time out of mind.
A Voice in the Crowd. Don't mince the matter, friend; we'll sit here till
The boat goes down, or we would miss a word.
There's no catcalling, only now and then
A squeak of conscience, as a frightened mouse,
While you plough up our dull, lethargic souls.
The Devil. I've been a travelling merchant of distress,
Cashed desperation; never struck a blow,
But when 'twas struck I pocketed the bruise.
I've fished up gains from streams of slain men's blood;
Ransacked the night for fetid oaths and moans
After a battle. I have bought the hearts
Of youthful lovers slashed with bayonets,
And hearts of geniuses that slight had crisped
Like frost-bit herbage, and philanthropists
That cunning policy had roasted; thirst
And hunger I have picked the marrow from,
And thrown the bones away; and pains from men

I've peeled, like tanner's bark, cords in a week.
'Twould take a month to tell of gluttonies,
And jellied whoredoms; men from rum-shops, pitched
Into the street. I've muckered round in lanes,
Ditches, and garrets, hovels, hospitals.
I am excited; I go for reform.
Your customs need to moult, come out bran new;
Mankind are saddle-galled, put on green leaves;
Down, down, below what you can see or hear,
The wronged ones quake with cold; let in the sun.
When Comfort shakes her children from her lap,
And Want doth wrench the shingles from your roofs,
The Times in pieces fall, like an old cask,
When Rich grow poor, and Poor are hutched with paupers,
All that men love, or hope, or wish, winds up
In hollow ruin; I go down with all,
Down to the bottom, grub among the settlings,
For that has been my avocation; wherefore
I can tell ye, there is no music there,

Nor dancing ; maidens never smile, but glout,
And stare at you like stupid walruses.
I wish I was a man like ye, I do,
Or had a tongue like one whom I heard speak.
But I've no soul ; yet in my kidneys, friends,
I feel these things are horrible ; and how
Men with souls can be calm, in such a pass,
Is what amazes me. Good night, farewell.

Philo. Annie, to thee, good night. 'Tis time you slept.

Midnight.

Annie. I could not sleep ; my berth was close and hot.

Philo. And so you risked the deck, at midnight, dear ?

Annie. With you there is no risk, for you are good ;
But why seek you no rest ?

Faith. He staid with me,
For I was curious to see the boat ;
And fore and aft we've scanned each part, while men

Have slept. The furnace, as a coil of lightnings,
One tended, adding fuel to what seemed
An earthquake-spring of fire, then wiped his brow,
And, calm as a child by its mother's chair,
He leaned against a post, and smoked and slept.
Along the gangways men were sound asleep,
On boxes, trunks, and the bare planks out-stretched,
As undisturbed as in their cottage beds.
Across the howling caverns of the main,
The pilot naively took the boat, as boys
Will ride a horse to pasture. This I ask,
If man can build and run a steamboat thus,
Shall aught to him appear impossible?
New modes of life, new forms of faith, new steps
In Time's old march, new looms in factories
Of Love and Truth, the Social Equity,
Pure governments, and all that's good and great?
Philo. Some Fulton now, I ween, elaborates
Your question; soon in splendid guise shall build
Ideas, through the currents of the age
Propel his novel craft, and error balk,

And wrong o'ercome by facts most palpable,
And gentle bravery of arithmetic.

Annie. The stars are out, all out; Heaven's Telegraph
By night. What the intelligence, dear Faith?
'Tis thine to spell the twinkling syllables.

Faith. It is the same old word, since time began
Repeated seven nights a week, GOD LOVETH!
That secret hath its thread within thy breast.

Annie. I guessed as much; while I have walked the deck
This dark and toppling hour, and felt what flames
Beneath us lie in wait, and seen what gulfs
Around us crouched, my heart looked up and said,
God loveth! Philo's arm about me stayed,
Assures the same; my fears upon that word
Are calm. Let fell disorder reign,
And whirl us to that dismal sepulchre,
Lashed face to face, we'd sink, sink to the stars.

Faith. They would receive thee as a little star,

Dropping from earth. Philo, this talk of stars
Suggests another piece of common fame, —
'Astræa Redux:' thou hast heard the tale.
Some call it superstition, yet I think
Such signs are pleasing.

Philo. I the pleasure own,
And superstition too; the omen hail;
Believe in Justice coming back to man.
This vigilance will steal away your strength,
Annie, if aught the weary week has spared.
You love me?

Annie. Yes, I do.

Philo. Obey me then,
And seek your berth, and I will mine; once more
Endeavor for a scantling sleep.

Annie. Two things
Rule mortals, love and sleep; be mortal too
To-night, sweet Faith, and come and sleep with
me.

Morning.

Annie. I wish I loved you better, Philo; then
I would be sleeping now, nor mind the rain.

Philo. Were you awake, you would see how unlike
Is rain to fog, which daintily detains us;
And thank me for the knowledge, albeit you loved
Me less. Bells, off shore, ring our cautious course.
Now rapidly the sun absorbs the mist;
The boat moves, we approach the river's mouth,
The gulls are screaming over rough Seguin.
The green firs show as spectres in the shadows.
Annie. There is Hydropathy in yonder rock,
Whereon the liquid snow-drifts plash; all baths,
Head, foot, and douche, in merry unison.
I'll join the aquatiles, when I can take
My medicine, insensate as that stone.
Philo. We'll get a party here next August; then,
I think, you'll like the water any way.
The rugged margin of the ancient Province
I can commend, and all New England too;
The grand old ocean here, and there man's safe
And fertile habitation; through the walls,
The smooth road runs, that never needs repairs.

The people crowd on deck, as to a meal,
And make their breakfast on the beautiful.
All love the Beautiful; remember that;
Scribes, pharisees, the shabby, the genteel,
Betokening descent from Paradise.
That fort is relic of the Revolution;
Last summer, on its grass-grown parapet,
I saw a cow reclined.

The Pastor. A thousand years
May she live and feed there, the only guard
Of our domain!

Philo. A mackerel boat! that risks
The main, and sits among the mermaid flocks,
Fearless as Faith in swells of human strife; —
The cradle of our seamen, bold and stout,
Whose bowsprits, as a shuttle, back and forth,
Shall web the ocean with our principles.
The region roughens near the sea, and springs
Continuous piers of gray, storm-weathering rock.
As we go inland, softer grows the scene;
The highlands shine in richer verdure dressed;
Embayed in green the thrifty farm appears.

Through forest-skirted ponds our winding course
Is laid ; and now a shrub-edged water-walk
We travel ; salmon-wiers we pass, and booms
Of logs, essays of our Lake-school of Poets.
Our steamer beating with a quiet pulse,
The beaded ripple crisping on the shore,
The clear-obscure of many a silent cove,
The steel-blue splendor of the stream, the sky
So blue above, the clouds voluptuous
And pure, like true souls in their hours of love,
And Annie here, with the angelic Three,
The birds that keep our joys in countenance,
These flourishing towns we see, and going home,
Our village elms, whose shadows wait for us ; —
All, all are beautiful, and beauty lies
With happiness and virtue in our eyes.

SCENE — *Within the Earth.*

Philo. To-day we take a subterranean road.
Charles. With rebel negroes in our fellow-ship?

Philo. The centre, cause, and end of Earth to
scan;
With power and method due from Gabriel.
Charles. Do we descend head-first? Enthusiasm,
Grown top-heavy, in stupid speculation,
Doth it turn upside down, and with its feet
Fling at the stars? Our visionary needs
Some lead upon his ankles.
Philo. By a step
And elevation old and wont we wend.
The door is high; this stone-pit, lately oped,
Our adit. Follow we this gneiss dip.
Charles. The path is crooked, turns are sharp and frequent,
Dikes intercept us, seam in seam is snared.
Philo. Beneficence of God. The strata cross,
And superpose, they brace and bind; hence strength
Of inward frame, and outward beauty, use,
Heights, plains, the busy stream, the sun-clad pond.
Charles. A silver mine! Soft you! Our fortune 's won.

This merest dust has some analogies
To Heaven ; — see, streets, trees, streams, gush in gold !
Charles. In faith, 'twill make our ball a lady-love,
And pietists will arm in her behalf.
'Twill disenchant Reform ; and Luther here
Would tarry, till the sun went down on Worms.
More sparkling in the gray recesses ! Earth
A pudding stuck with diamond plums ; — a slice
Our juncate-loving Poet sooth must have.
Philo. Here trip we on the roots of Pyrenees,
Here circumvent the pillars of the sphere ;
How rings the voice in this still labyrinth !
Charles. Is Hell more hot than Wedgewood's twenty score ?
Then we are on its confines, by my feelings.
Philo. What antre this, illumined from the sea
With dead-lights, as a ship ? I hear a sound
Of fire, and anvil-clangor ; — Vulcan's stithy ?
Annie. An ancient, venerable Form stands near
The forge.

Philo. It is the Genie of the Earth,
Whom Gabriel promised we should find this way.
Your servants, sir.
The Genie. I serve unserved ; the lone
And central slave and seneschal of all
This bulk of dust and passion, roots and graves.
I hammered on a wedge, as you came in,
To raise that British Isle ; it sinks a doit.
Charles. Its debt is heavy, not to say its preachers.
The Genie. To keep on even terms the land and water,
And foil the ocean when it crowds too hard,
Is all that me concerns.
Charles. That Lisbon quay
You swamped, a thousand shrieks extinguishing
In thousand butts of instant briny ruin.
The Genie. The vapors that perspire unendingly,
By pores innumerous, in every part,
Electric fluids, vital air, and others,
Infected in that outer human realm,

Returning by the Poles, are all drawn through
My fining pot, where I cleanse them with earths
Of subtile sorts, and sea water. The flame
And smoke at Stromboli and other vents
Discharge. It jars a little; never mind.
Your base is henceforth more compact and firm.
Besides, I see the currents every year
Come back less fusty.

Charles. Hope for you! dear Philo,
The breath of man is growing sweeter; dose
More alkali of blest Reform, your work
Is done.

The Genie. But these are trifles not worth naming.
In those old times, before your race was known,
It was no joggle, but a general mash,
And all the elements were by the ears;
No coast-lifting, but slam of continents;
America did tackle Africa,
Asia dowsed Europe, islands strangled straits;
And dark it was, so dark you could not see
Your hand before your face. The Animals

Were next produced, of that unseemly size,
Wrens condor-like, and asps like crocodiles,
Leviathan and Behemoth. They fed
On ling, and fattened in the reeky fens.
Through fume and fog the sun did faintly ooze.
In the warm sludge weeds grew to forests rank.
These orders perished; flesh and reed, in caves
I buried them, or strowed upon the land,
To brew the vegetable stimulus.
The ages mellowed, on the cycles flew,
Working incessant change in principles
And forms. I waited on the dissolutions,
Ground hills on hills, and mixed the various loam;
I strained the seas to dress the virgin fields,
Injected ores among the liquid rocks,
Smothered the thickets with the fiery mountains,
And sealed up endless granaries of coal.
I made a pretty spot for Adam, green
And sunny. 'Twould have ta'en your eye to see
The noble man, and gentle lady, Eve.
Fawns gambolled, linnets piped unto the lovers,

Clover and daisies all their walks besnowed;
And the good God said every thing was good. —
Folk should not build too near my chimney-caps,
Keep off high lava mark, look out for floods;
I rap the walls betime, alarum sound;
No fear of slumping in; you see what piers,
And solid groins, and porphyritic bonds.
I hear a blast, — they work an iron mine
I tucked away between the schist and slate.
Follow that path, and climb the rugged sides
Of Wales, and you will find it. Fare ye well. —
Philo. Here enter we the silent realms of Art;
Strong arms the pickaxe wield, some churn the drill,
Up slippery ways the loaded basket 's borne,
And lanterns shed a kindly ray throughout
This gloomy nether world.
Charles. The upper world
Is a more dismal mine in depths of Fate;
The Hate-damp there, the Fire-damp here, blast life
And light; all work in shade and end in slough.

Annie. One has a feeling of Infinity,
In this low spot, and church-wise worshippeth.
I should fear, Philo, if I did not love.

Charles. There's jollity withal, Anacreontic,
O'er ale pots, and Dutch scent of ham and krout.

Philo. Ride we up in the bucket, and pursue
This metal. Scores of lumbering wains conduct
Us to the Smelting House and Foundry. There
The cupolas in Theban pillars rise,
The slag in hills, unnoted on our maps.
Annie, go in, uncowardized by dust,
Or swarthy men, or creaking engines; bright
And plastic spirit doth inhabit here;
As clean as lightning in a reeky cloud
It shines betimes. The bellows roar with lungs
Of tempests, rings the dressing like a gong;
Some ram the flasks, and some the ladle drain.

Charles. The red-hot globules fly as if they were
Afraid of being burnt; your spirits gleam
Like dingy spectres with their sleeves turned up.

Annie. This man unearths a stove, all arabesqued,
And daintily inlaid with birds and flowers.
Philo. Its history forenote; that stove doth plait
The Borean zone with tissue of the Line;
Our snowbound parlors, windows intersprigged
With frost, it renders quite Arcadian;
It shelters poverty, and tends the sick,
Relieves the body, purifies the soul;
In winter nights those iron birds will sing
Unto our Poet, and the flowers distil
Castalian sweets.
Charles. Like taxes, toothache, tides,
A stove has no respect of persons. Once,
At a vendue, I saw a horse-faced preacher,
A skipjack transcendentalist, a lean
And muzzy artist, barbers, scullions, trulls,
Bidding against each other for an Olmsted.
Philo. Go we home and still ruminate our theme.
A nail — no nails, then no Phalansteries;
The covered walk and classic corridor

Come up from many fathoms under ground;
And powder, pulleys, hubbub, grime, and sweat,
Evolve the long-delayed Unity.
The knife that mends your most æsthetic pen,
A clump of ore, just tumbled from a cart.
Your seamstress' needle, packed with coke and lime,
Within the caldron seethes. The press that sows
Our Gospel, thick as sunbeams, on the world,
Is rifted from a ledge. Earth is a shell
Of spiritual kernels. Culture, progress, hope
Are troglodytal in their origin.
The iron rail and graded avenue
Behold! from Othosk to Seville; the phlange,
Now leaping rivers, worming now through hills,
Beareth the nuptial torch of Pole and Pole!
That cooper hoops the straggling empires. Earth,
Reaching from low, Plutonic depths, conducts
Her mottled children to each other's doors.
This budding orb doth open every morn,
And woo the maiden eye of Love. The Tree
Of Life beneath the wells of Artois sinks,
To junction of the hemispheres descend

Its roots, and marrow draw from fossil bones.
The prone is up, humility exalts;
On flashy pinnacles perdition vaults.

SCENE — *The Margin of a Forest.*

The Poet, (alone.)

Here is the rock, most opportune and kind.
I'll sit upon it; — lay my herbal there,
My fishing-rod stand here; fond wallet mine,
Most timely comforter, command my lap.
This flat-branched, wide-encircling beech shall shade
My head, and wait upon the pilgrim's rest.
How long, O Rock, hast been a settler here?
What storms hast weathered for the Poet's sake!
What pre-Adamic prudence scooped thee out,
Preparing me a smooth and easy seat?
When human vanities have sickened me,
I cleave to thee; when worldly promise balks,
Thy grit is steadfast; Friendship, Fortune, Fame,
Miscarry, thy support is good for aye.

In childhood's lavish years I climbed thy sides,
Leaped from thy summit; now, in middle life,
Gray hairs my head, and grayer thoughts my heart
Besprinkling, I would fain repose on thee.
David his harp enjoyed, I thrum a rock;
Petrarch his Laura had, I have a rock;
Our Pastor loves a horse, but I a rock.
When speculation wearies me, to thee,
O Rock, I come; aloose in dizziness
Of wild imaginings, I clutch thy base.
In hurly-burly of the times, thy crags
Thou liftest, stiff, serene. Though all things melt
In Ideality, or Anarchy
O'erwhelm the state, thy alumine endures.
These trees shall perish, empires, races, times;
O Rock, thou livest; shalt live when the birds
And every quick are silent in the dust;
Kind Nature's monumental tribute, raised
Amid the boundless solitude of ruin. —
What noise is that? What rustles on the leaves?
A dainty hare or brood of partridges;

Let me give chase: I will divide the game
Among my friends, and win reluctant bays;
Since viands flatter e'en if verses fail.
'Tis Wynfreda! my God, the Lady fair!
That white-robed lustrousness of womankind.
The same dark hair pours down the same white
breast,
The same fair hand sustains the same fair brow.
What dreams she? thinks she? What excursion
make
Her eyes? what meditation parts her lips?
Is it a spirit, captive in the woods?
Can flesh so counterfeit ideal stuff?
Shall I speak to it? Will it answer me?
Maybe a fancy of my o'erteased brain; —
O Rock, unspell me.

Wynfreda. Nearer, Poet-friend,
Come to me, lover mine.

The Poet. Be pitiful,
O Lady bright; do not elude my step,
Or mock my sorrows.

Wynfreda. I am sorrowful.

The Poet. Wilt not command a faithful ministry?

Wynfreda. The cup of vanity I cannot drink.

The Poet. Who, loving thee, would offer it? I kneel,
O Lady.

Wynfreda. Rise, sir, rise.

The Poet. I kiss thy hand.

Wynfreda. Thou mayest.

The Poet. Thou art mine.

Wynfreda. Thou art not mine.

The Poet. Mysterious woe!

Wynfreda. Mysterious woe!

The Poet. Thou canst
Resolve it. The perplexity is weft
Of thy own fashioning.

Wynfreda. From thee the threads
Are spun. — Ascend we to that glade; the flowers
Look out upon the sun, and there the earth
Respires expansive through the tangled copse.

The Poet. Thou wilt escape.

Wynfreda. Nay, do not hinder me.

The Poet. I cannot let thee go.

Wynfreda. Wilt not go too?

The Poet. Birdlike, before my aim evanishing,
How can I follow thee? how overtake
Thy misty step?—Let me withdraw: wilt thou
Come after?

Wynfreda. On thy track I oft have staid.

The Poet. O veiled, and beautiful, and much desired!
A shadow passing through the Poet's dream,
A cunning hint of solid good withheld,
A reminiscence irrecoverable,
Night-blooming, well-deep, bubble-swelling joy,
A wood-thrush note of hope, a cold, fair moon,—
O finger-tip embrace! O arms of sand!

Wynfreda. These expletives forego; thy passion wooes me not;
'Tis harsh and brief. Youth's first emotions need
A stint; must oaken up to manliness.
Can you sleep out o' nights alone, in cold
And haunted darkness of the world? intact
Of rheum and spleen, abide autumnal rains?

The frost must pinch the nut, or 'twill not sprout.
One cannot study in the sunshine; clouds
Are tutelary; trees late to blow are late
To fade. Thy first essays were rhyme, not rhythm;
Next rhythm, not song; then song, not Poetry.
In thy imagination some conceits
Went loose, as vesicles of air; and these,
Exposed in sonnets, were your prettiest smiles,
And classic sighs to catch your mistress' ear.
Your heart no living fire of Poetry
Engirded, you were not in blaze of love.
The simplers pluck our Poets in their flower,
Vapors to cure, promote euthanasy,
Preventing fruit and yellow harvest time.
Humanity doth rarely find its verse,
Except as musings in its castles hoar,
Or idyl sunshine on its rustic vales.
After a shipwreck, music of the bard
Is heard up in the mountains, as relate
Those Grison peasantry. The light of him
Of Newstead, burned as camphene lamps, diffused
A graceful shower of soot all o'er the globe.

Inhabit life as eremites their cells ;
Foray, as bees ; assotte your generous ends ;
Dam Nature's streams, and fill the idle flumes
Of Progress ; through the ice-blocks of a dull
And stagnant form in sparkling crystals shoot ;
Load with your wares the vacant wharves of
thought ;
Grow up an Epic ; even let your feet
Disclose your royal birth, as once a prince,
Whose rustic guise had else deceived his captors ;
To El Dorado, Martinez was led
Blindfold ; advance, albeit your way is dim.
In this swift, bell-toned brook, I thee baptize.
And, Poet dear, I've known thy works and ways,
Have seen the gift divine ; yea, more than gift, —
The nature, power, and virtual element
Creating thee ; the Poet of the Poet's self ;
Covering thy diction bald with glossy curls,
And chiselling thy taste to fairest moulds ;
Seen thee turn sawdust into allegory,
Beauty discover in a green baize coat,
Render just meed to honest affluence,

Extend thy arms to hostile opposites,
And hook the broken chains of interest,
Patient with ignorance and pedantry ;
In riding, with the driver sit, and save
The landscape, and economize the road ;
Find life in charred stumps, and culture fetch
From the new settlements.
Ah ! Poet dear,
I languish in environments ; my gyves
Are wearing me in slow suspense away.
On thee my ransom 's poised ; thy gallant truth,
Thy earnest depth, thy troop of well-drilled
verse,
Alone can conquer that which conquers me.
A waiter-woman, gross and vile, is set
About me, brutish wealth attempts my hand.
This bandit circumstance thy melodies
Can shake, and end my sensuous alarms.
My heart thine pants for, thine my love espies,
No other flatteries shall me distrain.
Yet seek me not ; the forest fell, — as flowers,
I spring up in thy path ; break down the walls

Of dominant disdain, and I am free ;
And every where we'll spread our bridal couch.

The Poet. O Lady fair, how long ?

Wynfreda. To-day, to-morrow.

The Poet, (alone.) 'To-morrow !' This forenoon, and yesterday,
And everlastingly, O Rock, art thou
At hand ; thy ready flint bespeaks me comfort.
On thee the wronged Indian wept his fate,
On thee dismated finches troll their griefs ;
Shall I too weep ? The grass is green about,
On this harsh surface soft the mosses lie.
Sternness and immobility, O Rock,
Give me, that still shall bear some gentle thing.
Withal, be ballast of my honest pen,
As, overhauled, it puts to sea again.

SCENE — *Parlor at Annie's.*

Annie. Tell me of what befell your recent jaunt.

Philo. The Alleghanies we ascended, there
Composed exertion, and refreshed our heat.

We drank those bubbling streamlets, that, four-
cleft,
Descending either flank, inundant, gleam,
And intervein the vast imperial fields.
A stranger vision challenged our regards, —
It was the Genius of America
From the Blue Ridge appearing ; slow he rose,
And solemn, as a saint, with prophet beard,
And broad and marble brow, discovering half
His form, and half immixed in cloud. His hand
He waved, and people gathered unto him.
The nation, personal or legatine,
Was there. The sunny South and fertile West
Poured forth. From Accomac the rally came,
Presque Isle and the Old Bay and Mackinaw ;
They packed the vales, and mantled all the hills.
Music the deep and vivid silence eased,
A choral hymn, from the thin air it pealed,
And effigies of angels were the singers.
Then prayed the Genius, fervently and rapt,
As Moses prayed for Israel in Sinai.
Repent! — such was his text — God's kingdom
comes.

Americans, immortals, men ; discoursed
He thus ; Ye Pilgrim sons and Huguenot,
Or sprung from polished loins of Chivalry,
Archprimates of the realm, Precedency
Potential, give ear ; ye are sinners all,
Highgoing, inexculpable, confessed.
The fulness of events in Jewry 'gan
Ye hinder. He, your Lord and King, would come
In clouds, in clouds of summer beauty dressed,
An over-cloud of new Transfigurement,
His Truth investing, as a lambent flame,
Your dwelling-places, on your hills his Love
Dawning a golden Orient. Revealed
In you, his face would shine afresh, and Earth
Reflect the Son of God ; his Advent be
As lightnings, flashing from the eyes of men.
Ye sin and darken all the life divine,
Smother the rising brightness of your God.
The face of Jesus, personal in you,
Ye smut with murders, drunkenness, and strife ;
The road where he would make triumphal entrance,

Cumber with fierce dragoons and gangs of slaves;
Your spirits, that his own would beautify,
Ye mire in passions vile; rejecting crowns
Immortal, trick yourselves in spoils of office.
Ye wage a war more foul than Lucifer
In Heaven; he broke with God, and so have ye;
He did not sell his fellows; that ye do,
And push by arms your worse than devilish trade.
Ye build with Rome, with Rome ye must go down;
Ye copy ages past, with them are plunged
In one perdition; bastions rear to fall
In vengeful crash on your own heads; disown
Jehovah's name, and trust in man's device.
The just ye ostracize, the honest scoff,
True patriots supplant with sycophants.
Palmyra's dust already strows your streets,
Your history is gathering leprous spots,
Your robes of empire smell of charnel mould.
Dear people all! ye know not what ye do;
How hope in all the earth for you is troubled;
The Westward Star declineth in its place,

Perplexing earnest eyes that sail by it.
Beneath you coal-beds lie, — of what avail?
In every acre is a priceless pearl, —
Who heeds it? Think upon your ways, reform
Your doings. Give the Indians homes, enfeoff
Those nomades; free your slaves; unhand the soil.
Repent and shun dismantlement of doom;
Few years have done for you the work of ages,
By forelock ye have ta'en degeneracy,
And copied ills ye had not time to grow.
Ye ministers of Christ! how dare ye thin
Eternal truth with weak expediency,
And tickle prurient ears with feathered words,
Raise dust in eyes of a pursuing God?
Repent! let renovation work, and your
High Destiny speed on; your Gothic force,
And plastic energies, accelerate
The Chiliad of Hope and Prophecy.
Your sea-gates to the nations wide unfurl,
Your Rocky Mountains turn to lithophanes
Of freedom; Northern Lakes for fountains bore,
And here a jet appoint, whose skyward flight,

Recoiling liquid arcs and gay colures,
Shall charm the sight of millions, and revive
The desert face of this great nation's virtue.
Charter your navy for the voyage of love ;
Disband your armies, or in mercy's name
Commission them, to help the beggary
And close the springs of vice your rule creates ;
Your revenues, in schools, arts, parks, disburse ;
Raise a millennial arch, through which the Lord
Of this Young World, and all his train of grace,
May pass. Thus spake he, handling themes like these.

Annie. In what complexion stood the multitude ?

Philo. Some said an Angel spake, and some, the Gods
Were come to dwell with men ; some marvelled if
These things were so. The slaves, throughout the grounds
Dispersed, applauded, while their masters ah'd
In silence ; Indians rose majestical,
And many whites slunk abject at their feet.

A pompous commodore did grind the sward
With his boot-heel, as if beneath him lay
The seven deadly sins, and he his rank
Forgot to crush the vipers. One cried, Treason!
That word, Actæon whelp, to his own soul
Returned; he went pale, panting, thin, and fell
Beneath the fanged onslaught of his sin.
A politician rent his hair, and wept
Forthwith the music sounded long and loud,
Reverberant through the clear breadth of space,
As the celestial circles twanged unseen,
And touched the surly core in every breast.
Meanwhile, above the horizon appearing
From woofy clouds that doze on summer hills,
Defiled the Genii of every land.
In sackcloth part, and part with rotted girdles,
Others were veiled. Within his arms one nursed
The Vestal urn extinct; one bore half-furled
A faded gonfalon; while four sustained
A pall; one with a star was crowned, the star
Of the Nativity; on his white lips
Another pressed his finger wistfully.

The foremost clutched his beard, and fired his eye,
Black and severe, among the gaping host.
Outspoke he thus: Americans, beware!
From graves of nations are we come, to yours
If ye will have it so. For headstones stand
The ages; running to the birth of time,
In shadowy lines, the mouldering columns stretch.
Are ye deceasing? Shall we gather up
Your eagle-flag, through endless wanderings
To bear it in our melancholy arms?
The Evil Spirit lies in ambuscade
Among these States. Americans, beware!
Direct, our Eagle, slowly drifting, came
In sight; he halted, backwards wheeled, ensnarled
His stately spires, as if he were besot;
Relaxed his talons, let the arrows fall;
Fitful he sprang, by lurches swept aloft,
As he would dash against the sky and perish.
Down dropped he, feet first, with his pinions shut,
Down like a bullet; now, his poise regained,
He darted off afield, and disappeared.
Returning, in his beak an olive leaf

He bore. The Genii acclaimed so loud,
The echoes doubled in the nether world.
These visions vanished, and the people all.
And while I gazed, the day being nearly spent,
Faith, Hope, and Love, the holy Trinity,
As three snow-bodiced schooners on our coast
Were wafted by, in midair floating on,
These circuiteers swang noiseless on the wind,
The twilight shimmering their muslin vesture ;
As if the anxious land had laid its head
To rest, and they kept watch about its bed.

SCENE — *The Air.*

Love and Nemesis.

Love. O Night-nursed, sin-hunter, proud Queen of gloom,
Put back. Anoint thy wiry locks ; an couldst,
Thou wouldst be jovial ; do smile for once,
Give thy eternal frown a holiday.
Nemesis. Delay me not; behind the pack are yelping, —

Fire, Famine, Pestilence, and Anarchy.
Canst sop the thunder? Will damnation coo
And bill you as a dove? Thou know'st the Law.

Love. Multipotent in pain! thou art not chief.
'Bove woe, and me, and thee, there is a God;
He willeth not perdition, but reform.
Wilt be before with him? Didst thou invent
His thought? If of his counsel, know he grants
Us grace; his Son has pleaded, judgment stays.

Nemesis. Have I not seen, not heard? Canst thou divert
The scent of trained vengeance? Why are owls
Abroad? What means the raven on that pine?
Precursive sickness blasts the needful crops.
E'en goodness' self cries fury on its foes,
And ravaged innocence bemoans to heaven.
How long hast been awake? Thou wert asleep.
What tares, midtime, were sown, thou wottest not.

Love. Methought I woke to hope, and not despair.
Auspicious hands aroused me; better days
Seemed near.

Nemesis. Fond hoper, thou art drowsing still!
In thy forbearance, Love, the globe itself
Would spoil, its arid rocks with vermin swarm.
We cannot trifle, stop to prick the sleep
Of gluttons, sow catarrhs in thin-soled shoes.
We come the age to scourge, and execute
The races, nations, lands.
Love. The whole, in bulk,
The fresh-toned child, and brazen sin of man,
Do thy intentions, indiscrete, impeach?
Nemesis. The babe is fattened on inhuman milk;
The wooden-sworded stripling hath the vice
Of Cæsar; ruffian banners are emblazed
By velvet-fingered girls. E'en terms are lost,
And language hath revolted. To invade,
They call protection; maintenance of right,
Is perpetration of all damning deeds.
Cathedrals shake with gory canticles;
Depauperation gallops into town
On back of sleek and well-fed opulence.
Why aid the scandalous engendering,

Transmit the venom to posterity,
Go pandering between the faithless years?
Let death arise, and forfeit life devour,
Let havoc smite the fabrics of deceit,
And chaos calm the long and godless strife.

Love. O atrabilious, sour-eyed kith of doom!
The light blinds thee, as an untimely bat;
Thy Acherontic sense distastes a rose.
Wert at the Deluge, didst not see the Bow?
Hast never heard of Calvary's sweet blood?
O, awful Justice! deer-foot Retribution!
Do not hard-mouth me so; hist there thy dogs;
They gnash on me; I give thee no affront.
I too have seen and heard. — Incensive man!
His guilt is great, too great for estimation,
Beyond punition, haply; baffling thee,
Like dead men's dust. — Give ear, O Pursuivant!
There are who painfully bemoan the times;
Repentance sobbeth as its heart would break,
Remorse doth cut the vital force of lies,
In sin's broad way a deep alarm hath spread;
The Hopeful put their hands unto their ears,

And hearken for the sound of wheels, not thine,
O Ineluctable, but his, the Prince
Of Peace. Stand by, thou mighty Fate, and let
A Mightier exert his saving arm.
With fuller's soap he shall our vileness wash,
Our constitutions thresh, and fan our state;
Through greed, and craft, and lust, and hardest rind
Of our besetments, leading up to life
And light our aspirations; smoking flax
Of sorrow he'll not quench, or break the reed
Of tender virtue. Stern, sublime, give way;
Thy presence will our noble women fray.

SCENE — *A Winter's Ride.*

Philo, Annie, and Spirit of Love.

Philo. Wilt ride with us? a school intendency
Takes me abroad.

Love. The purpose pleases me.

Philo. Our Winter 's kind, though rigorous and long;
Its discipline is good, and works in us

A lasting and a noble energy.
Within its terms, as in its icicles,
Is beauty too ; and singular delights,
With every sort of social harmony.
This season brings our produce to the market,
And loads of richest thought to every mind.
The brook runs free and clear beneath the ice ;
The soul, in furs, has a pellucid face.
What railroad can surpass this glittering track ?
The horse's feet spin pleasant roundelays, —
A winter-bird that chirrups in its flight
Is this our swift-sped runner. See those sheep ;
They keep an open foot-path through the snow,
Narrow, and winding, as a forest walk,
Down to the spring, at bottom of the field ;
True seekers, humble, patient, undismayed,
They trudge along, and never mind the weather

Annie. There is a leaf, that yellow, autumn leaf,
Dear Philo, on the snow ; it trembles, starts ;
Away it goes, and in a thicket hides.

Love. For ages, Annie, such my lot, to skim

Across Siberian surface of the world.
The Day is coming that shall melt all hearts ;
In sweetest dissolution I shall die,
Still being vital in the life of all.
What house is that ?

Philo. 'Tis an Inebriate's.
The rafters through the roof, like Hunger's ribs,
Are splitting ; in the wind, the clapboards thwack,
As they would drum up Hell its carnival
To hold on this debauched farm.

Annie. The hens,
Poor things, have lost their legs, or use but one,
As 'twere a crutch. Is that result of drink ?

Philo. Their feet they pocket in their wings to warm.
Shall we go in ? Upon the hearth is sprawled
The man, or husband, so in law behight ;
The woman we met going for more rum ;
Yonder their son hacks at an apple-tree
For firewood. Winter doles no blessing here ;
The Sabbath is a bane ; all thrift enures
In folly ; the essential blood secretes

Blains, fits, and purulence of heart and will.
These lips, like Libyan sands, are ever dry,
This carrion attracts calamities
In flocks. Before us, God's blest image lies
A malt-worm.

Love. Is this irremediable?

Philo. Some hold the law catholicon. Alas!
The appetite unquenched would dram the winds,
Intoxication sift from all the bolls
Of nature. Culture, ministries of good,
A varied recreation, milder cups,
Enfranchisement of all the faculties,
A temperate conscience, loyalty to God,
Are indispensable.

The road again,
And mountain freedom of the air. Our way
Through walls of Parian lustre grandly runs;
We cross the woods that nurse their sap in silence;
Black fences rim the alabaster meadows.
Harbored in a dense forest, close upon
The street, the red school-house you see. The
boys

Have built rude palaces of snow, the girls
Are sliding on the ice; down yonder cliff,
Some wildly leap and tumble in the surf
Of this their transient sea. They leave their sports,
Still sporting to their books. Let us go in.
This does not match with Eton, yet are these
Our princes of the blood, the best we have.

Annie. Your royalty is gristled in its prime;
Your Dukes have hands as tough as walnut bark,
The little Duchesses perambulate
In boots, stout, heavy, as a fisherman's.
Truly, here's fine iconoclastic stuff —

Philo. Some grains of which will not be out of place.
But, soberly, that girl, in woollen 'tire
And frowzled hair, hath a poetic mood,
They say.

The Schoolmaster. What mood? Not one of Murray's five
Knows she, and none of just subordination.

Annie. Speak to these children, Love.

Love. Be not too strait,

Good friend; your pupil's confidence command,
His will is yours; 'tis passion frights all thought,
While gentleness encharmeth application.
And, children dear, be orderly, and mind
The rules, and so your teachers shall mind you.
I came from God, — do not be startled, — Christ
Came from the same; I am no more than he,
And have no other words. In Holy Book,
Upon your desks, he speaks; will you hear him?
There, children, speaks the Good to make you good;
There waits the feathered heart to brood on you,
As tender chickens; full of tears his eyes,
That you may never weep; his hands are torn
With thorns, where he pursued his wandering lambs.
The wine cup utterly refuse, be fixed
Against all war, combine in truest love
With the brown boys of Tartary. Grow up
Purely, as checkerberries in your bogs,
As bright and beautiful in heart and life
As your fir thickets in a dewy morn.

Lift, boys, your little sisters o'er the swales,
And, girls, do merrily your mothers' wishes.
'Tis in your power to make your rural homes
As seats and dwelling-places of the Angels.
But yesterday an Evil dire I saw,
Whose shadow broad, as if the sun were lost
In irreversible eclipse, bestrides
The total earth, and these green-wood abodes.
Be you good, so this Evil, as the winds,
Shall pass, and you be saved from that great woe.
Adieu, dear children; love, and all is well.

Annie. Do not the teachers, Philo, need tuition?

Philo. Most sure they do, of schools, the Church, and all.
Unction they want, and not certificates.
Baptize the mind, and love on genius rain;
Verily the Scholar must be born again.

SCENE — *A small Burial Lot, enclosed, and set with Trees; other Graves; a River near.*

Annie. 'Tis Charles; I see him through the trees; he stands
Rueful, by the sad shrine of his lost one.

Philo. Shall we go to him?

Annie. Softly loose the gate.
A soothing silence reigns throughout the spot;
The elms condole with every mourner here;
Murmurs the river pensive in this shade;
These monuments look forth as spirits mild
Congealed with sorrow; our Madonna droops
As if she never felt a woe like this.

Philo. The first bland voice of Spring has called him forth,
Receding snows reveal the fatal mound,
The grass revives, but not to him revive
The joys of parentage; the sparrows sing;
That sweeter music, which a child's whole life
Evolves, he cannot hear. Our Pastor comes,

From stroll among the new-warmed lairs of buds.

Annie. Hast not a word for Charles? Of all your flock,
Is he outcast and lost?

The Pastor. He knows no God,
He owns not Christ. The trees are gemmed, outflash
The maple blows; his sap, refractory,
No vernal heats affect, his principle
Of life is doubt-bound, fast in rigid atheism.

Annie. I see a gentle sunbeam on his head,
And lovely Spring is warming at his heart.
O sir, he has some feeling; how it lifts
And agitates that lump of dark despair!

The Pastor. It is an ice-quake, peradventure, not
The loose and mealy fracture of the soil.
And yet, to feel is crude, atomic life.
He loved his child, and gods in flesh are children.

Philo. We're not usurpers of the hour, dear Charles,

Or place; that both enforce their will with us.
I went with Annie through the greening gully,
Riparian transports kept us on our feet;
Hither, you know, we could not fail to come;
With you, we feed our tears on this charmed dust,
As yours, our willowed spirits droop with grief,
And wave funereal above your dead.

Charles. Your kindness, Philo, is a cheveril stroke
Across my aching head, albeit the twinge
Continues. I am glad to clinch your hand,
Because you clinch me back again. I love
This spot, where yet each breeze that I inhale
Is spined with sorrows; every morn I rouse
My woes that every night I rock to sleep;
I miss my child, and seek where she is not;
I rake her ashes her blue eye to find;
Her dying finished me, and still I make
Her die again a dozen times a day.
There's Annie's rose, — that too is winter-killed.

Annie. Nay, Charles, look you, the inner bark is green.

Philo. A voice so long contemned, so long unheard,
Our Pastor's, jars it on your present mood?
Charles. I'll not say, yes; he is sincere, therefor
I like the devils.
Philo. Were he good withal,
With double warrant he might claim your ear.
He is a father, and has lost a child.
Charles. Let me observe the cadence of his tongue,
I'll sense his quality. You, Annie, call
Him here. — She is an angel, only one
That I accredit. Any gift from her
Were sanctified, e'en in canonicals.
The Pastor. I know your lack of faith, and strength of love,
Things incompatible, so strangely joined,
As if a dove were brided to an auk.
You, Charles, are greater maze to me, than death
To you. Have never children died before?
Shall none die after? Are not we in weeds?

Did love begin and end with that rare birth?
Does no Divine the human interfold?
Blind-drives the Universe, gruff, hollow, dark,
And recks it nought for your deep agony?
Is not our love immortal? Time or place,
Or all divertisements, could they induce
Oblivion of the rose-cheeked innocence,
That crept your floors, and glee'd your garden through?
And what is this but Supersensualism?
What fascination in the haggard turf!
What transcendental beauty in the tomb!
To you, who rate as one most reprobate,
An unknown river, verdurous and calm,
In drear and troubled coasting of the soul
Doth open; mounts your child, and wins the sire
To Heaven; attempts Eternity, and makes
A breach where you may enter. Your delight
In that unpeered progeny, was it
A ganglionic fever? Swells your grief
But to collapse? Yean annual ewes, soft bud
The gnarled oaks? — has travailing love no due

And lineal afterpart? Were Nature's means
Exhaust? Could she no longer keep your child?
Has God no darlings? O ye little-faithed;
It is the pleasure of the All-Love, you
To give the Kingdom. Meekly wait for him.
Snatch not the dawn, keep to your couch until
The ruddy bliss feels after you, and fillips
Your slumbering lids. In quietness revolve;
Solstitial hours draw nigh, thy Norrland wilds
With crocus-breathing gales shall gladdened be.
The Church door 's wide, go in; disconsolate
Are Holy Mother's care. And others, Charles,
Will weep with you, and teach you how to praise;
Pure sympathies before the Power Supreme
Shall blend, a white-armed sisterhood, and move
In choral volt to piety's sweet stops.

This end-all, Philo, hath a self-relief.
Bereavement hallows many a barren wold,
God's acre 's held in universal fee;
Through death to life is a perpetual round.
The worm's papescent, Hades is a garden,
Silence matures in amaranthine bulbs,

Our stagnant blood, in honeysuckles, steams
Nectarean, through the humid evening air;
Genius doth lessons take of stark decay,
And executes in these unfading glyphs.
And I have walked with death as with a brother,
Communion taken such as life affords
Not every day. Dust elevates above
My dust; and pearl-browed Peace 'mid sable scenes
Comes forth, as on a battle field the Moon.
Doth Heaven's orbit graze the grave? How else,
Standing on this low tump, bathe I my head
In joys unseen, how else does this heart beat
With tumult of contiguous seraphim?
 What sore distress this spot comprises, Charles,
I know full well. There lies our child, our pet,
Her dimpled fingers, and her dear caress,
A prattling bellibon, our hearth's best warmth;
And there the choicest, purest of my herd;
Beyond, a cultured soul, rare-gifted thought,
And closest fellow of my mind; the next
Was sage and ancient counsellor. I am
Not old, but I have buried more, most dear

To me, than some whose age is mewed in wrinkles.
If friendship be perpetual youth, the Pastor
Soon sinks in years, and grows untimely bald.
Affliction thins his sides, fate gives a staff
Whereon his young decrepitude must lean.
Adieu, constrict, hope-lorn; Christ weeps with you;
Those tears purl through your sorrows and create
A vale of beauty in that bleak domain!

Charles. He did not tax my frowardness, or plant
A feather in the way of freest thought.
I'll go and hear him preach next Sunday, see
Where leads this new ignescent intimation.

Philo. Singing their key-note close to them, stout cups
Of glass, we break. Your heart's key singeth he;
Would God that heart might break, and truth come in,
With joy and peace; eternal life begin!

SCENE — *At Philo's.*

Gabriel and Philo.

Gabriel. The Day approaches, yonder steeple-
top
Is gilt with rosy dawn. My work is closed;
Preliminous on these events, I staid,
Still urging consummation of the hour.
The Angel of the Trump hath sounded, wide
The volleyed peal hath startling clanged; the press,
And pulpit, and the lecture-room, repeat
The word in kindling pulses through the land.
Poets have sung, historians moralized,
Conventions sat in judgment on the race.
The graves are opened, and the dead come forth;
The silent catacomb of prescript wrong
Is rent; from dust of forms and empty rites
They rise to life; lust, an unfathomed sea,
Gives up its dead. His vial on the earth,
God's undiminished wrath, an Angel poured;
Confederate fraud and pampered cruelty

He smote ; on hurtful governance and laws
There fell a grievous sore, and plague of hail.
Fabrics of sin are scorched with sevenfold heat ;
Spirits unclean still work foul miracle.
But brief their course ; the two and forty months
Of rampant Blasphemy are almost run.
The obstacles of custom, prejudice,
Mountains and islands, flee away ; your Cause
Its free wave rolls as an eternity.
Daughter of God, and mother of pure souls,
Conscience, — the Woman, driven out, pursued
By floods of bestial malice, — reappears.

Philo. What noise hear I ?

Gabriel. Applause that welcomes her.
The stars of titled might and bloody fame
Are falling ; lo ! their odious splendor quenched.
Listen ! in the tops of the mulberries
You hear the sound of going ; 'tis the Church,
That travaileth as cleaving mountains sore ;
'Tis Virtue's hosts that march through Achor's valley,
Furbish the spear, put on the brigandine,
And strike for Armageddon, where resides

The King, Expediency, and a hard fight
Is threatened. See! they search Jerusalem
With candles; lights flit to and fro in halls
Of office, cabinets, and the exchange.

Philo. What rocks our base?

Gabriel. The adamantine bands
Of manifold oppression, girthing states,
And weighing on the people, burst; and burst
The chains of slavery; and prison-walls
Of all Injustice part, as part the spheres.
The heavens and the earth shall shake, and men
Shall know that God is sovereign of the world.
Behold the beams Christ's Coming flings before,
Dwellers in darkness crowd the Eastern shore!

The Advent.

Philo. The bell has tolled, the starting signal 's given;
A band of music plays our solemn flight.
The white scarf streaming from thy raven hair,
And buttoned with a rose-bud, well becomes

The Day, and thee, dear Annie. Glorious Day!
No morn so bright; the clouds are Beauty's gift
Withal, impearling the cerulean.
And for this fête of ages, all in white
Are dressed. The cattle graze rorifluent meads;
The lumber-men have doffed their suits of red;
The river, unopposed by pothering keels,
Flows Sabbath-wise; the foam, in fleets, glides soft.
Our town's folk rise, from all their gates they rise,
And take the air; vehicular winds transport
These Western watchers whither the New Star
Directs; above our house they buoy, and pass
The hills, as feathered squadrons from the pole.
Dreadless mount we the Glory-destined car.
Where He beheld the kingdoms of the earth,
Upon that Mountain high, 'tis fixed for him
To be revealed; all kindreds, tribes, and tongues,
Confluent thither, gather unto him.

Annie. This zephyred transit, winged voyaging,
Quiring like orbs through the ethereal fields,
Unspeakably delights me; and with thee,
Dear Philo, in whose soul all goodness lies

Aërial, where I, for many a month
A leaden sinner, nursed my pinions small,
And taught my purer essence how to soar.
Sweet smell the pastures, sweet the groves of pine.
The Earth hath washed in musk and lavender
To greet the Day. Behind us, Faith and Love
And Hope, three swans, are swimming. Groups appear
With sprigs of christmas-rose, and some with palms.
Blue-ribboned girls sing on their flying march.
Abreast by twos, the Clergy go, their albs
And bands were ne'er so white before. Who those
With open collars, and a hunter's frock?

Philo. They are Reformers.

Annie. In the midst of them
I see the Wandering Jew; and on my troth,
There's Charles, the Ishmaelite; does he believe?
The Poets pass; I know them by their curls;
Their hair streams orphical, as they dash on,
Like merry skaters, through the glary void.

Philo. Lo! on a sea of glass, 'mid fire-like rays,
As if the falling stars still quenchless burned,

The victor sons of Virtue, harping, go,
And sing the song of Moses and the Lamb.
High up the lucid coast, an Angel stands,
With rainbows crowned, and feet of glistering
flame,
Who swears the time is over, and the end
Of hidden mystery of God is nigh.
Forth gallops one on a pale horse ; 'tis Death
Of death, a valiant champion of life ;
Quarter of earth he subjugates to Christ ;
His fervor kindles, gleams his golden shield.
Annie. Yonder horizon darkens on my sight !
A caravan of shadows traverses
The plain. What is its omen ? Had I wist !
Does disappointment mix with all we do,
And with this Day, like salt in the salt sea ?
As from a pit they rise, as Styx had swarmed,
And colonized its horrors ; leopards winged,
Girl-headed locusts, folk satyric born,
Lathy and crank. A woman leads the rout
Sitting a scarlet horse ; while dragons trail
Behind, and howling time the sullen march.

Philo. War, Slavery, Intemperance, are those,
The Evils, Bigotry, Monopoly,
Oppression, others that infest the world.
That Woman, chief, is War; no woman she,
A thing of terrors, fetor, madness, wrapped
In mantle of a witch. I met her once
Before. Let no uncertain thought arise.
They are disabled, and reserved in chains
For Judgment great and terrible of God.
On, on, the people billow; their white vests,
Like a slant snow-storm, fleck the amber vast.
A thousand leagues an hour we make; and now
We verge the spot appointed; now the lines,
From East and West and North and South, unite,
In eddying cadence, close the Mount around.
On grassy seats, prepared by Gabriel,
Aslope, the shining ranks arise; a host
No man can number. Lo, He comes! our Lord
And Christ; he comes to judge the world; or, more,
To let his truth exert judicial force,

Dividing soul and spirit, joint and marrow.
The halo crowns his uncrowned head; a Name
Is written on his vesture and his thigh:
THE LORD OF LORDS AND KING OF KINGS. A light
That pales the solar fires, his face emits;
The ready faces of his followers
Repeat the radiance, blush an equal flame,
That threads with lightning touches the concave.
The Sisters three, in nebulous mutation,
A cloud-glory, impendulous, adorn
This pageant, and his Coming dignify;
Anon to merge in the Eternal Beauty.

Annie. Who those that at his feet lie low, and seem
In tears to smile, and smiling still to weep?

Philo. They're Poverty and Ignorance, and all
The catalogue of Innocent Distress;
Thousands of thousands, won from dens and caves,
Mountains and deserts of their varied woe.

Annie. To his left hand the imps of darkness turn;

They maunder, gloam, and cower intimidate
Together, cower before his blasting eye.

Philo. As on a balcony, preëminent,
Distinct with rarest splendor, carved or wreathed,
By art of him, van-courier of the Day,
Justice and Mercy sit; sweet Mercy, fair
And young forever; Justice, dread, severe,
Hath shed her terrors, glows as fair, as young,
And holds a bunch of gladsome heliotrope.
From empyreal distance mist-like come
The harp-bearing Seraphic choir, and loose
Their light-weft cinctures to the beamy winds.
He speaks; the hushed collective ear attends.

Christ. Empires, men, brothers! my design ye feel,
And instincts of the highest hour obey.
Occasions infinite, immediate,
Within you work, God's moment touches you.
Celestial salutations welcome you;
My heart doth welcome sons and daughters here;
Enter into the pleasure of your Lord.
But listen to the rendering of time,

And what report, to mine afflicted ears
Your Consciences have immemorial borne.
For ages hath this blessed light at gates
Of morning knocked, and with its dew-bent locks
Waited in silent suburbs of the world:
Admission ye refused, the sin-obscure
Preferring, and licentiousness of night.
The Prophecies, of old communicate,
My hope and promise, often uttered when
I sojourned in the flesh, still unexpressed
By you, sole medium of heavenly grace,
Have been as things that were not; often glossed,
But never lived, or in your lives fulfilled.
I would have come in mine own church, revealed
My glory in the fire of pulpit truth,
And virtuous action: how that fire ye dulled!
I should have dwelt in you, and ye in me;
From your eyes, I have all too faintly shone;
Your heart with my celestial purposes
Hath rarely moved, and when I would have walked
To visit prisoners and liberate

The captive, heal the sick, your foot disdained
Its office. Ye vouched me your Guide and
Head
With sacrament and populous attest:
But when I bade you bless your enemies,
Ye cursed and killed. I bade you live in peace,—
The clash of arms, and tumult of affray
Have swept incessant discord round the earth.
You named me Wisdom, him a fool who kept
My words; Atonement, and with God and man
Fomented wasting, everlasting jars.
My simple laws and genial sway ye flung
Aside for corporate brutalities,
And false, despotic state of selfishness.
Erewhile, the brightness of my Coming had
Consumed iniquity; that mighty force,
Not mine, but God's, in you distort, corrupt,
Hath given itself to the support of sin,
Enforcing the supremacy of wrong.
On my left hand, what Monsters ye have reared,
What fed on dainty croppings of your guile,
What from your loins have ignominious sprung,

And what, in basest aspect, ye yourselves
Have been, behold! God lays no measures hard,
Or hard to be discerned. He loveth you;
Ye were dear sons and pleasant children all,
And he would dwell with you, walk in your midst.
And me, his Son, your Way, and Truth, and Life,
He gave; nor lacked there ought for your perfection.
I came to save, and still to save am come.
I will not heap reproach, nor need I add
To what your quickened apprehensions feel.
Is this your sin well charged?

The People. The awful guilt,
O Lord, we own.

Christ. Shall't be destroyed?

The People. Amen,
So let it be; the execution haste.

Christ. Almighty Love, bright effluence of God,
Essence of mortal or immortal hope,
Thou purging rapture and detergent joy,
Hidden too long, but not too late made known,

Now glorified with glory of the Son,
Shine forth! with thy transcendent vigor shine.

The Phantasms of the Evils. Hide us, ye rocks; on us, ye mountains, fall!
The day of wrath is come; and who can stand?
Flee we from Him that sitteth on the throne.

Chant of the Seraphic Choir. Rejoice, ye nations, and his people all!
He renders vengeance on his adversaries.

The Kings of the Earth. O Lord, confession cannot magnify
What yet thy grace exceeds — our sinfulness.
Imperialty disgraced by us thou wilt
Extol; we cast our crowns before thee; be
The throne and sceptre thine. Our governments,
Long traitorous to thy supremer reign,
Return to thee. Our subjects, wronged, in wrong
Ensampled, cheered to hate, from love withheld,
To knowledge shut and hope, by levyings
Forespent, be thine to rule; thy subjects we.
Our nations join to virtue's wide domain.

Chant of the Seraphs. To Him, their Prince, the kings of the earth bring
Their glory, and in his light the nations walk.
The Politicians. Thrice terrible in thy great beauty, Lord!
Can mercy measure such a guilt as ours?
Thy brightness shows how vile we be, alas!
So vile, what floods can cleanse? No height so great,
No deep so low, of infamy, but we
Have traversed it; thy chosen scoffed, pursued
Thy saints, perplexing the Redemptive plan;
Have interlined the sacred page with lies,
With lies have filled thy prophets' mouths, the right
Postponed to pretexts of the passing hour,
Bargained away the hope of every age.
Our collow souls, who sees but to despise?
And thou 'fore all. What penance wilt impose?
To kneel on rocks, or fasts or vigils keep?
Can hard contrition wear away these frauds,
Hypocrisies, and pensioned villanies?

Have mercy on us, Son of God! and as
Thy Coming brightens, let our spirits clear.

The Transcendentalists. In homage, due to goodness, Lord, we bend
To thee, who Goodness art. O Wonderful
Of the create, O Miracle of time!
Thou curdled breath of rare divinity,
Thou soul of Virtue, globed in human eyes,
Eternal Word on ruddy lips incarne!
Too oft on self we gazed, and less on thee:
To-day the mirror 's broken; let it lie,
Since God through thee and us is shining fair.
We would no friend or brother; after us
Thy mother eyes went streaming; flowers the dew,
Harts drink the water-brooks, and we ourselves,
More sweet to us than Jewish muscadine.
Our fount ran dry, alas! good Lord; and now
We bring our empty bowls to thee. We shone,
But inward, oven-suns, none blessed our light;
Lord, bless us; we will bless, unsought, unspent.

Bishops and Clergymen. Repentance, Lord, we've urged, how little felt!

Submission, arrant rebels to thy word;
Thy sovereignty professing, still controlled
By passions of the populace; and awed
By human statutes while we played with God's.
With forms the spirit ridden, simple truth
Entoiled with web of curious subtilties.
Thy people lay as wax beneath our hands;
Failing thy lustrous image to impress,
The lines of sect, and our usurped estate,
We drew thereon. But why augment our shame?
Thou knowest, Lord, the direful summary.
Baptize us with thy fire, our spirits purge
With thine own holy spirit. Man-ordained,
Renew our ordination; take our robes,
And clothe us with thy righteousness. When thou
Art gone, in us thy living face be seen;
To bliss supernal welcome us at last.

The Pope of Rome. Thy function, Lord, and virtual sanctity,
We've held, imposturous; betwixt thy Church
And thee, a carnal governance have thrust;
The mitre overshades the Cross, our will

Thy will defaults. The key of knowledge we
Restore to thee. Shine on thy church, through us
Outshine. Be Head entire, and we the feet.

Chant of Seraphs. The priests do gird themselves, lament, and weep;
The altar-ministers in sackcloth lie;
The Pastors fold again the scattered sheep.

A Multitude of Men and Women. In us be glorified, O Lord, from us
In living waters flow. Thy love and works,
And life and death, by us be manifest.

Christ. Depart from me accurst, adulteries,
Unnatural affections, heresies,
Wrath, murder, unbelief, idolatries,
Abominations, whatsoe'er defiles
Or makes a lie, in unquenched fires consume.

Chant of Seraphs. Glory to God in the highest,
On earth peace and good will to man!

Angel of Prophecy. This is the First Resurrection.

Chorus of People. Resurrection's morn has come,
Souls emerge from night profound,

Ages burst their silent tomb,
  Years of God begin their round.

Prophecy fulfils its moons,
  Earth in Christ transfigured lies,
Nature all her winds attunes,
  Human modes accordant rise.

Heroes come from battles won,
  Shades of martyrs o'er us bend,
Zion gleameth as the sun,
  Empires Virtue's heights ascend.

Crowd the chorus, swell the lay,
  Lift the shout of Jubilee,
Hail, exultant, hail the Day!
  Shake the hills with ecstasy!

Philo. From God's throne and the Lamb's, a river runs,
As crystal clear; the silver cataract
Down steeps of azure falls; encompassing

The vision, far the level gleam extends.
Bosquets of Health-Trees picture its bright lane.
The Twilight and the Dawn descend and bathe
Their ancient sheen in the rare-tinted depths.
Christ. My grace be with you all, and love of God,
Communion of the Holy Ghost, amen.
Philo. The Day is finished, and thereafterward
Comes no night. Virtue reigns eternal noon.
Gabriel ascends to other spheres. As stream
Into a stream, as flame in flame is merged,
Christ flows into humanity, and lights
The body of the world; all eyes look him,
All lips declare; the lineaments divine,
As stars incarcerate in emeralds,
Ray from the whole environment of man.
Annie, where are our friends?
Annie. On yonder cliff,
The Poet with the Poets sits, their souls
As with some ocean-glory, swelling, gleaming.
Beside him, Wynfreda, her glowing hand

In his, a lily on the same wave rocked ;
She droops toward him, and from her eyes I see
The glory-flood responsive tears distilling.
Peruses Charles the sacred Mount, where His
Receding lustre like a foot-print stays.
Through polyglottal throngs, 'mid shout and song
And dance, go Edward, Julia, Henry, Sarah,
Meandering, as through belligerent states
A river, giving beauty unto all,
Beauty imbibing. Choirs of clergymen
Of every order, with our Pastor sing
Te Deum !

Philo. List ! The Wandering Jew to us
Is beckoning ; points he to a cloud of smoke
Careering from beyond that hill. We will
Go with him.

The Wandering Jew. Tophet burns, and in it burn
The Evils.

Philo. Holiest incendiarism !

The Wandering Jew. A hand unseen is busy here, and breath

Of God doth tind the place. In sulphur flames,
War crisps and shudders like a burning feather.
Intemperance with all her crew is drowned
And dissipated in that lake of fire.
Fast to a stake with her own manacles,
The fagots blaze about the Dragoness,
Fell Slavery; a hissing tempest beats
Oppression down; the carcasses of Lust
And Avarice are broiling; Slander gnaws
Her tongue; Deceits like adders wimble through
The singeing vapors, and expire; Force falls
And Hate in the conflagrant vengeance. — Lo!
The fires go out; the Sun, all genially,
Shines on the ruin. You behold what look
Like substances, a damned group of things;
Dead ashes all, dead, dead, and the first gust
Will scatter them. And now, good friends, rejoice
With me, — I am a man, and have a soul;
I felt it thrilling up my flesh when He
Was on the Mountain, that old soul of my
Long-sundered youth. This rare decomposition
Shall work productive affluence. This spot

I'll occupy; 'twill please you still to think
That Tophet is a farm, and he, yclept
The Devil, farmer too. The best of hay
These horrors will afford. In cherry-time,
Hither your children bring, and they shall find
The vilest ills may yield the choicest fruit.

Philo. God! who from darkness brought this world to light,
From darkness still to light dost bring us on;
With our own wickedness correctest us,
With our backslidings dost reprove! Our sins
Into the depths are thrown, the wilderness
Breaks forth in waters, parched ground in pools,
In dwelling-place of dragons springs the grass.

Annie. Here, Edward, flashing gladness, hastes to us.

Edward. The wonder, Philo, has but just commenced.
The world entire is a great hive of blest
Commotion. Scattered to their homes and posts,
The people all are working out the sign
And import of the Day. Come you and see.

Annie. Ringing of steel I hear, and echo-crash,
As million sledges smote a million anvils.
Philo. You closely paraphrase the fact. Their swords
To ploughshares, spears to pruning-hooks, they beat;
Nor ever blacksmiths gave such lusty blows.
They rend the forts and whoop down citadels.
The slaves are frolicking; to-morrow they
With freeman's will a freeman's work will do.
The alcoholic fire in fire goes out;
A mob of Adventers the gallows touze;
See bands of exiles singing to their homes;
Scrimp jails to airy hospitals arise;
Cities exude their poisons, as a fog;
The mephitism is banished by the winds.
The Cumberland road, with many wagon loads
Of reparations for the Indians,
A mirthful rabble crowd. There is a town
In Phalansteric change; the houses move,
As trees of old, to sweet synergic pipes.

See gardens multiply, and bulbs increase,
See tasteful cottages adorn the plains.
Our senators eventful progress feel,
And meet to Christianize the constitution.
The epoch deepens, wide our God hath rule ;
Beyond the seas prophetic crises thrill.
Love balances their power, and soothes their fears ;
Their ships of war convoy Millenial rapture
Around the earth ; the serf to burgher mounts ;
The lazzaroni weave in factories ;
The Moslem is agape, and opes his mosque
To Gospel preachers. The glad news spins on
To Ispahan, and shakes the Chinese wall.
Enough for one day ; let us homeward wend,
And in our hearts the solemn lessons tend.

SCENE — *A Bower in Annie's Garden.*

Philo and Annie.

Philo. Early among your flowers.
Annie. So are the birds.
We were so fledged with glory on That Day,

So Morn-informed, the birds expect a mate
In us. I've brought you out a rose that bloomed
While we were absent, a Prince Albert that
I waited for; as fragrant as our bliss,
And beautiful as Jesus' flowering.

Philo. Your rose denays the ancient god, and gives
Us speech, so keeps up with the time; and love,
In roses eons dwelling, finds a tongue
At this late hour.

Annie. Make me an olden rose;
I will keep silence while you speak.

Philo. That Day,
That Coming, that Recension, whate'er
It be; — grant it a vision that we both
Did see, call it a dream we both have dreamed; —
There is a Spirit-death, and Spirit-life;
And this is the First Resurrection; such,
Meseems, is the decisive Gospel sense.
Christ comes in us, and quickly comes, if quick
Received, for centuries has yearned to come.
He died to sin, that we might die, and live

Again. With him we buried lie, with him
To rise. Is he a Judge? e'en so are we.
Smote He the world with the rod of his mouth?
That mouth are all who his plain truth express.

Annie. What is the Second Resurrection, or
The Second Death? Hereafter, what the doom
Of wickedness and unrepenting men?

Philo. If it so be that goodness hath no charm,
The will is kerned in impenitence,
That vice with irrecursive, Pontian flood
Sets in, and guile and hate shall organize
The nature; if so be that sin is soul,
And soul is sin, without a flaw between,
Or seam impierceable by sword of truth,
Then are not both to the same pit consigned?

These speculations by the by. — The News,
The Glory-day, the Evangeliad
Of ages, occupies the mind. Christ saves.
The earth brims with a pure enthusiasm.
Hilarious all and holy. Heart to heart
Its signals hoists, eyes dawn on eyes, the streets
Redemptive look, the folk Redeemed. Watch we

And pray, and daily trim our mortal lamps.
Regeneration is the work of life ;
The blade, the ear, the full corn in the ear,
Is still the law. The trellis deftly set,
What hinders Earth from climbing to its God ;
Whilst down the arbored void the purple fruit
In the long summer centuries shall hang,
And children on the mountain tops will pluck
The Good and True, as I this bunch of grapes.

The minor tale a marriage often rounds,
And on the greater a new lustre sheds ;
Nor are Divine events too great for that
Wherein Heaven is foreshadowed — nay, doth orb
Itself about us, and within us spring.
Annie, let this glad week our gladness crown,
Be Bridal of the Church and Christ our own.

THE END.

COMPLETE
LIBRARY OF NATURAL HISTORY,
ILLUSTRATED WITH
400 ENGRAVINGS.

This work was carefully compiled by A. A. Gould, M. A., from the works of Cuvier, Griffith, Richardson, Geoffrey, Lacepede, Buffon, Goldsmith, Shaw, Montague, Wilson, Lewis and Clarke, Audubon, and other eminent writers on Natural History.

It is all comprised in one imperial octavo volume of about 1000 pages, handsomely bound, and is in itself, as its title indicates, a complete library on this subject. Price $3,00.

SHAKSPEARE'S
DRAMATIC WORKS;

Complete in seven volumes, imperial octavo, of nearly 550 pages each; forming in all nearly 4000 pages. The above edition of the great dramatist is known as the "magnificent Boston edition," being celebrated for its transcendent beauty of typography; and in this regard altogether the finest American edition extant.

PROVERBIAL PHILOSOPHY,
A BOOK OF THOUGHTS AND ARGUMENTS ORIGINALLY TREATED.

BY MARTIN FARQUHAR TUPPER, M. A.

First and second series, complete in 1 vol., 12mo, with fine portrait, and bound in the various styles of plain, full gift, &c.

THE MECHANIC'S TEXT BOOK,
AND
ENGINEER'S PRACTICAL GUIDE;

Containing a concise treatise of the nature and application of mechanical forces; action of gravity; the elements of machinery; rules and tables for calculating the working effects of machinery; of the strength, resistance, and pressure of materials; with tables of the weight and cohesive strength of iron and other metals. Compiled and arranged by Thomas Kelt, of the Gloucester City Machine Company. Complete in 1 vol., 12mo.

To the careful mechanic, the above will be found a work of invaluable daily reference. Price $1,00.

BIOGRAPHIES, &c.

Life of George Washington,

Commander-in-Chief of the American Army through the Revolutionary War, and the first President of the United States.

BY AARON BANCROFT, D. D.
Illustrated with Engravings. 12mo., Muslin, $100.

LIFE AND CAMPAIGNS OF NAPOLEON BONAPARTE;

Giving an account of all his engagements, from the *Siege of Toulon to the Battle of Waterloo*; also, embracing accounts of the daring exploits of his marshals, together with his public and private life, from the commence ment of his career to his final imprisonment and death on the rock of St. Helena.

Translated from the French of
M. A. ARNAULT AND C. L. F. PANCKOUCKE.
Numerous Engravings. 12mo., Muslin, $1,00.

HEROES OF THE AMERICAN REVOLUTION;

Comprising the Lives of Washington, and his generals and officers who were the most distinguished in the War of the Independence of the United States; also embracing the Declaration of Independence, and Signers' Names, the Constitution of the United States, and Amendments; together with the Inaugural, First Annual, and Farewell Addresses of Washington. Four Portraits, 12mo, Muslin, $1,00.

PICTORIAL HISTORY OF ENGLAND,

BY HUME AND SMOLLETT.
Abridged and continued to the accession of VICTORIA.
BY JOHN ROBINSON, D. D.
Engravings, 12mo., Muslin, $1,00.

The Life of our Blessed Lord and Saviour Jesus Christ;

To which is added, the Lives and Sufferings of his Holy Evangelists, Apostles, and other primitive Martyrs.

BY THE REV. JOHN FLEETWOOD, D. D.
Numerous Engravings, 12mo, Muslin, $1,00.

PILGRIM'S PROGRESS,

FROM THIS WORLD TO THAT WHICH IS TO COME.
BY JOHN BUNYAN.
With Notes, and a Life of the Author,
BY THE REY. THOMAS SCOTT,
Late Chaplain to the Lock Hospital.
Illustrated, 12mo, Muslin, $1,00.

MUSIC BOOKS.

White's Church Melodist.

A new Collection of Psalm and Hymn Tunes, adapted to the wants of Choirs, Singing Schools, &c. By Edward L. White, Editor of "The Modern Harp," "Melodeon," "Sacred Chorus Book," &c.

American Collection;

OR, SONGS OF SACRED PRAISE.

BY EDWARD HAMILTON, ESQ.

The greater portion of the music in this book is *entirely new*, and of a very high order; and Choirs will find it a rich accession to their musical libraries.

Congregational Singing Book;

OR, VESTRY COMPANION.

The music in this book is composed entirely of old choice standard tunes, such as will be familiar to all. They were carefully collected and edited by Asa Fitz, Esq.

Common School Song Book.

This will be found to contain a very choice collection of simple, and for the most part, familiar airs, beautifully adapted to the wants of *Juvenile Choirs*, the *Private Circle*, or the *School Room.* Edited by Asa Fitz, Esq.

Sabbath School Minstrel.

This little volume is especially adapted, in its Music and Hymns, to the service of the Sabbath School. It has been much admired wherever it has been used. Edited by Asa Fitz, Esq.

Greek Course of Studies.

Crosby's Grammar of the Greek Language.
Crosby's Xenophon's Anabasis.
Crosby's Greek Lessons; consisting of selections from Xenophon's Anabasis with directions for the study of the Grammar, Notes, Exercises in Translations from English into Greek, and a Vocabulary. The above are already in very extensive use in the colleges and classical schools, and are very highly recommended.

LIBRARY EDITION

OF

STANDARD POETICAL WORKS.

IN UNIFORM STYLE.

TUPPER'S POETICAL WORKS; embracing Proverbial Philosophy, Thousand Lines, Geraldine, Hactenus, and Miscellaneous Poems. Complete in 1 vol., 12mo, muslin, fine portrait, Price $1,00.

COWPER'S POETICAL WORKS; with Life; a new edition, 1 vol., 12mo, with portrait. Price $1,00.

POPE'S POETICAL WORKS; new edition, containing a Life of the Author. Price $1,00.

BYRON'S POETICAL WORKS; with a Sketch of his Life, in 1 vol., 12mo, and embellished with a portrait. Price $1,00.

MOORE'S POETICAL WORKS; an entirely new edition, in 1 vol., with portrait. Price $1,00.

BURNS'S POETICAL WORKS; embracing a Life of the Author, Glossary, and Notes. A new edition, 1 vol., 12mo, with fine portrait. Price $1,00.

SCOTT'S POETICAL WORKS; with a Memoir of the Author, embellished with a portrait. Price $1,00.

LIFE, GEMS, AND BEAUTIES OF SHAKSPEARE; all embraced in 1 vol., 12mo, containing six fine engravings and portrait. Price $1,00.

POETICAL REMAINS OF HENRY KIRKE WHITE; containing a Memoir of the Author, with an introductory chapter on his religious and poetical development, by Rev. John Todd. Price $1,00.

LIBRARY EDITION
OF
STANDARD POETICAL WORKS.

IN UNIFORM STYLE.

HEMANS'S POETICAL WORKS; an entire new edition, in 1 vol., and illustrated with steel engravings. Price $1,00.

HOWITT, COOK AND LANGDON'S POETICAL WORKS; a new edition, 1 vol., 12mo, neat muslin. Price $1,00.

MILTON AND YOUNG; containing Paradise Lost, and Young's Night Thoughts, a new edition, complete in 1 vol., 12mo, with portrait. Price $1,00.

CROLY'S BRITISH POETS; combining the beauties of the British Poets, with introductory observations by Rev. George Croly, 1 vol., embellished with fine steel engravings. Price $1,00.

THE POEMS OF OSSIAN; a new edition, containing ten steel engravings, and printed on fine paper, 1 vol., 12mo. Price $1,00.

THOMSON AND POLLOK; containing the Seasons, by James Thomson, and Course of Time, by Robert Pollok, complete in 1 vol., 12mo, with portrait. Price $1,00.

WORDSWORTH'S POETICAL WORKS; an entirely new edition, from plates just stereotyped, complete in 1 vol., 12mo, with portrait. Price $1,00.

CAMPBELL'S POETICAL WORKS; including his Pleasures of Hope, Theodoric, and Miscellaneous Poems, many of which are not contained in the former editions. Complete in 1 vol., 12mo, with portrait. Price $1,00.

The above poetical works are uniform in size and binding, and are sold separately, or together. Their size and style considered, they are the cheapest library editions of the same authors before the American public.

www.ingramcontent.com/pod-product-compliance
Lightning Source LLC
LaVergne TN
LVHW050513100826
845148LV00002B/324

* 9 7 8 1 4 2 5 5 2 1 5 1 6 *